# HELL'S DOORWAY

Bronco Grant knew the Brimstone country better than any man, apart from his Apache sidekick, Running Dog, and even he was scared of the mesa called Hell's Doorway. When two hardcase hunters hired him to take them hunting in the Brimstones, Grant figured this was the answer to his financial problems. Soon he was working down in the bowels of the earth, held hostage and forced to do exactly as he was told. There had to be a way out – either through the blazing guns of the men who had brought him there, or through the doorway into hell itself...

# HELL'S DOORWAY

Bronco Grant knew the Brimstone country better than any man, apart from his Apache sidekick, Running Dog, and even he was scared of the mesa called Hell's Doorway. When two hardcase hunters hired him to take them hunting in the Brimstones, Grant figured this was the answer to his financial problems. Soon he was working down in the bowels of the earth, held hostage and forced to do exactly as he was told. There had to be a way out—either through the blazing guns of the men who had brought him there, or through the doorway into hell itself.

# HELL'S DOORWAY

*by*

Clayton Nash

**Dales Large Print Books**
Long Preston, North Yorkshire,
BD23 4ND, England.

British Library Cataloguing in Publication Data.

Nash, Clayton
    Hell s Doorway.

    A catalogue record of this book is
    available from the British Library

    ISBN   1-84137-021-5 pbk

First published in Great Britain by Robert Hale Ltd., 1998

Cover illustration ' Faba by arrangement with Norma Editorial S.A.

Published in Large Print 2000 by arrangement with Robert Hale Ltd.

Dales Large Print is an imprint of Library Magna Books Ltd.

Printed and bound in Great Britain by
T.J. (International) Ltd., Cornwall, PL28 8RW

X000 000 031 2162

# PROLOGUE

## The Way Into Hell

In late 1864, the war was winding down and the Confederacy was preparing for its last stand, facing inevitable defeat but aiming to go down fighting and with whatever honour could be salvaged from the years of death and misery.

That was why it was so important that the two wagons got through with their hidden cargo.

One was a Connestoga, the other a Studebaker, much lighter and slimmer than its companion. Accompanying the wagons were a dozen outriders dressed in rough frontier clothing, looking like the Westerners they were supposed to be, but at least two had a certain military look about them.

The first was obviously the leader, a beefy man in his thirties, scarred and weathered with either a sabre cut or a tomahawk slash across his right cheek. His hair was long but his shoulders were squared-away; his jaw thrust out and his eyes raked the country around him constantly.

The second man was rawhide lean and dried-out, with a beak nose and brown tobacco stains in the deep lines running from his nostrils either side of a thin mouth to his jawline. He chewed and spat and occasionally dropped back alongside the other riders, checking them with hard eyes.

Anyone could spot this was an army operation, despite the attempt to make it appear nothing more than a band of buffalo hunters taking their stinking hides to the nearest town or trading post.

The nearest town beyond these Brimstone Hills was a hundred miles south-west and not much of a place anyway. Certainly there was no railroad to ship out the hides that filled both wagons. True, there was an old trading post closer, but to the north – and the Yankees had almost reached that point in their sweep deep into the South, so it wouldn't make any sense to take the hides there.

Major Harris could pass for someone who had come from north of the Mason-Dixon Line. The rawboned, tobacco-chewing man could get by as a borderline Yankee, but the outriders were boys from Carolina and Louisiana, with a couple from Tennessee and one from Texas. Hard to disguise accents that went with those pedigrees.

Harris dropped back to speak briefly with the rawboned man, Sergeant Magill.

'We're nearing Indian country, Lije. Tell the men to check their guns and spare magazines and so on.'

Magill squinted at the officer, spat a stream of brown juice. 'You see somethin', Major?'

Harris hesitated. 'Maybe a flash on that rise yonder.' He tilted his scarred jaw in the direction of a small mesa. 'Could've been a mirror or sun flashing off the lens of a telescope. But we have to cross that mesa.'

Magill nodded. 'I'll see to it, sir.'

'Lije – forget the courtesies of rank here. We've a long way to go yet and you could make a slip in some bar.'

Magill nodded. 'Long habit, s– I'll watch it.'

Harris smiled faintly. 'You're a good man, Lije.'

Magill's face showed nothing of the small pride he felt at the words. Once again he thought how strange it was to hear an educated voice coming out of that battle-scarred face. The scar on Harris's face was his souvenir of Gettysburg. Some said he'd fought in the first battle of the war, was first man in his town to enlist, leaving a good position at some college to help push back the Yankee menace that threatened his way of life. His folks were supposed to have owned a plantation somewhere near Atlanta, now he didn't even know if they or his young wife were alive or dead.

That was one advantage Magill had over the officer: there was no one to grieve for him if he was killed, and he had no one to grieve over, either. Made for a better fighting man, he always claimed....

An hour later, as the wagons slogged their way up on to the small mesa, any thoughts of loved ones – or lack of them – were pushed violently out of the riders' minds.

They were just mounting the last of the steep trail when the Indians hit with their usual cunning ferocity.

The teams were sweating and straining, exhausted, plodding step after step as they fought the last few yards towards the level ground. The men were busy shouting, urging, cursing, some out ahead with ropes tied to their saddle-horns, pulling the heavy wagons to help the struggling mules.

Only Harris and Magill took time to look about them in case of attack, but the sergeant was occupied with the Studebaker which had hung-up a rear wheel on a rock, when Harris yelled.

'Oh, Lord save us! They're coming!'

Every man's head snapped up and bellies tightened as hearts leapt wildly when they looked in the direction Harris was pointing.

Indians were coming from everywhere it seemed, ahead, sweeping in a wide arc, riding out from behind house-size boulders, dropping over the rim. Then there were war-whoops from below and the men, pale now, twisted anxiously to see more coming up the narrow, winding trail, trapping the two wagons and their riders neatly.

There was nothing else to do but fight.

These men had been hand-picked for their devotion to duty and the Confederacy. They would fight to the last man.

Although they were outnumbered almost three to one, there was one thing in their favour: the Indians had only a few guns. Mostly they were armed with bows and arrows, lances, tomahawks and war clubs.

But they would fight fiercely just the same when there was a chance of picking up firearms from the white men, especially

Henry repeaters. The disguised soldiers were veterans of many battles, and several had fought Indians before. Best of all, they were good shots and their first volleys, in front and behind the wagons, killed several, causing the Indians to break off their reckless charge, sweeping left and right on the mesa while those coming up the trail had nowhere to go.

'Get rid of those red bastards behind us!' yelled Magill, firing his massive Dragoon, seeing the ball split open a screaming Indian's chest, punching him clear off his horse with its impact. There was no hope of turning the wagons or going back: they could only press on towards the flat of the mesa, but at least if they drove off the raiders behind them, they could then concentrate on those ahead.

Gunfire rolled and echoed from the eroded slopes of the mesa and a fog of powdersmoke drifted downtrail. When it cleared enough to see, the narrow trail was strewn with dead or writhing bodies of both men and horses. Those still alive and mounted, turned dangerously and rode over their downed comrades as they tried to run out of range. The Indians afoot threw themselves over the edge of the trail and slid and rolled and somersaulted down to the plains below. Magill roared for another volley and some of those fleeing were picked off.

It wasn't the kind of fight Indians liked, seeing their companions blown apart by heavy calibre balls from big Spencer carbines and Henrys, but they wouldn't give up easily when these weapons were the prize. Those in front suddenly charged and the guns cut a swathe through their ranks, scattering them across the mesa.

While they regrouped, Harris and Magill word-whipped their men into getting the wagons up the last steep slope of the trail. They had barely heaved up five yards on to the flats when the Indians swept in again. Harris could swear they had doubled their numbers – they must have had reinforcements waiting amongst the rocks.

It would be slow work getting up any kind of speed with the laden wagons, but once they were rolling it would take more than a thin line of screaming Indians to stop them.

Harris bawled at the drivers to whip-up the sweating teams.

The Henrys and Spencers thundered and rattled and mustangs and warriors ploughed into the mesa's hard ground. The iron tyres rattled on the packed earth and this helped the wagons gain speed quicker than Harris could have hoped.

The Indians fell back before the hammering lead, but they waited until the wagons and men had drawn level with their positions and came thundering in again, whooping, showing these white-eyes the master horsemen they had to contend with.

They slid to one side of their racing mounts, clinging with iron-muscled legs, firing bows beneath the arched and straining necks of the mustangs.

And some of those deadly shafts found their targets.

Two white riders went down, hitting hard, rolling, coming to rest in tangled heaps, unmoving. One man reared up screaming in pain as an arrow pierced his upper right arm, shattering the bone. Another tried to snap off the shaft protruding from his right thigh, lost balance and fell. Two more arrows pinned him to the ground. A third stood in the stirrups, clutching a shaft that stuck out both sides of his neck. He rode like that a few yards before pitching out of leather.

Magill himself felt the smashing thrust of an arrow in the back and then he was going forward, somersaulting over his mount's neck. He hit the ground and the wild-eyed horse thundered right over him, falling and skidding. But Magill didn't move, the arrow driven completely through him.

Sweating, Harris hastily thrust a tin loading-tube into the butt of his smoking Spencer and glanced at the wagons. The drivers were standing in the seats, the canvas covers behind them pierced by arrows and a few Indian bullets. Other arrows quivered in the wood frames. One mule had a shaft sticking out of its rump and he knew it wouldn't be long before it went down, the wagon would crash and...

They were thundering along close to the northwestern edge of the mesa. He knew the down-trail lay more to the west, tried to direct the drivers, making wild cutting signals with his arm, yelling orders. Then...

Without warning the ground opened up beneath them.

Harris watched, bewildered, eyes bulging as he saw the wagons sway and lurch, falling backwards and sideways at the same time. His horse whinnied, reared in terror.

He had no idea what was happening, only that *the world seemed to be falling away beneath him!*

Dust erupted in choking clouds. Huge clumps of earth and rocks crumbled underfoot. Men, animals and wagons all spilled wildly into the dark pit that yawned beneath them like some monstrous maw, opening to engulf them all.

Even as he dropped into a roaring, dust-choked darkness, he saw his other riders tumbling headlong, some Indians, too, and the sky above fell rapidly away as the earth swallowed the entire wagon train.

His last thought was that they were all falling into hell.

## 1

### Brimstone Man

They called the town Brimstone although it was a good two days' ride from the mountains of the same name.

It was the only town anywhere near the rugged ranges and the seat of Brimstone County, of which Fergus Perry was sheriff. The town had come into being after the war when the Reconstruction saw a need for a headquarters in this region of Colorado. It was now on the Sierra and Prairie Line spur-track, fed by freight and passenger trains alternately, week about.

Ranches and farms of various sizes were scattered around the rich though rugged country between the town and the distant hills and they all used the railroad to their advantage when they had call to.

Like Bronco Grant, working owner of the Busted G spread which, having failed at raising cattle, was now having small success as a horse ranch. Grant had the reputation of being a fighter and it was said he knew the Brimstone Hills better than anybody, and that included the Indians, who still prowled there in this year of 1881. Bronco Grant could disappear into those hills with his Apache sidekick, Running Dog – called simply 'Dog' – for weeks at a time and, when he reappeared, he would be driving a bunch of horses with coats gleaming with fitness and health, ready for market.

No one knew how he managed to track down so many fine animals, busted them to the saddle back in the secret canyons, and drove them contentedly and willingly down to the rail depot holding pens outside of the town. Others had tried, had gone bust trying to locate big enough herds or ones with good quality animals, and a couple had even gotten themselves lost so that Grant had to go looking for them. He had brought them out alive every time and these accomplishments added to the growing legend about the man.

But this warm day in early Fall, Grant was in town to pick up a shipment of harness buckles and metal saddle frames: he made his own tackle and much of his leatherwork was sought-after as far away as Montana. He had made several gun holsters and belts and was now receiving more and more orders for these through the mail. He made a point of lining all his holsters, and sometimes the insides of the belt rig, too, with suede, and it seemed that the idea was fast catching on with men who needed – or thought they did – to drag iron in a hurry.

He had noticed the man with the squared jaw and friendly face lounging outside the barbershop on his way down to the depot and the man had nodded to him casually as he built a cigarette.

Grant, a tall, easy-moving ranny, weathered the colour of a rifle butt by the

Colorado seasons, lean and big-boned, saw the man was still leaning against an upright of the barbershop awning as he came back along the narrow boardwalk, toting his heavy package of tackle findings. There were some new metal stamping tools and edge-cutters also adding to the weight.

As he neared the stranger, noting now the man had heavy shoulders that strained at the seams of his checked shirt, and that the big hands rolling another cigarette were scarred and showed signs of having busted knuckles in the past, Grant shifted the package to under his left arm.

He executed the motion just as he drew level with the man and somehow the package jostled the stranger's elbow and he spilled tobacco and cigarette paper into the gutter. He swore softly.

'Sorry, friend,' Grant said, with an easy-going drawl, the sun catching his three-day stubble and highlighting some of the silver-grey hair scattered amongst it. 'Here – have one of my cheroots.'

The friendly man – well, he didn't seem all that friendly of a sudden. The square jaw thrust out aggressively and the calm blue eyes narrowed, the head leaning forward on a thick neck that showed rigid veins.

'S'pose I don't want one of your goddamn cheroots?' he demanded.

It startled Grant some and he frowned, catching sight of a couple of men just going into the barber's pausing abruptly and looking sharply at the stranger.

'Well, in that case, I'll put it back in my pocket and be on my way.'

One of those big, broken-knuckled hands reached out suddenly and he felt the steel grip of the fingers on his upper left arm, preventing him from moving.

'You just gonna walk away?'

Grant held the man's cold gaze a moment and then nodded gently. 'That's what I aim to do, friend. I haven't the makings and you don't want my cheroots, and I've apologized. Can't see the point in hanging about any longer.'

The big man shook his head slowly, looking around him with mild exasperation. 'Whole blame town seems to be the same. No one gives a damn. Your barber made me wait for a trim and shave, wouldn't even set me down right away for a silver dollar tip.'

'Well, that's the way things are in Brimstone,' Grant told him warily, seeing there was a lot more danger in this man than he had first thought. 'We wait our turn for things.'

The man showed strong white teeth in a tight grin. 'You tellin' me I'm impatient? A bully, mebbe, forcin' my way in where I ain't entitled?'

Grant felt his muscles tightening. *What the hell?* This *hombre* was prodding him, crowding him into a fight...

'You've a knack for putting words in a man's mouth, mister. Must've gotten you into a lot of trouble in the past.'

The tight grin widened slightly. 'All the time. But I don't mind. I kinda like trouble.'

Grant shook his head and made to step

around the man. 'I don't have time for trouble today ... too damn busy.'

The stranger deliberately stepped into Grant's path, spread a hand against his chest. Grant heard the men standing in the doorway suck in sharp breaths. Other men were drifting down, curious now.

Grant looked down at the hand pushing against his chest, flicked his hard grey gaze to the man's expectant face.

'Why're you crowding me, friend?'

'Why're you pussyfootin' about? You know we're gonna fight. Why not get it done?'

Grant frowned, stood very still, studying this man. Yeah, he *wanted* a fight, all right. And seemed it just had to be with Grant, no one else... That was what intrigued the bronc-buster. Why? he wondered. He had had enough fighting in the war and since had gone out of his way to avoid as much as possible in civilian life. Not that he ran away from trouble, just avoided what was unnecessary. But no man would crowd him without good reason and, once he drew the

23

line in his mind, he didn't back off, not one inch.

And he had just drawn the line here with this big stranger.

'You got a name?' he asked suddenly, startling the man.

Then the big man said, 'Just call me Chick.'

Grant nodded. 'Got a notion you already know my name.'

Chick smiled. 'Bronco Grant, hoss-wrangler and Injun-lover. They say you're a squawman, too, with mebbe three or four of them Injun gals tucked away in the hills an' that's what takes you back there so often.'

Grant smiled thinly, shaking his head. 'Save your efforts, Chick. You don't have to work at prodding me any more. I'll fight you.'

Chick blinked, not used to men accepting his challenge so readily. Then Grant dropped his heavy package on Chick's left foot and the man howled and leapt back in pain and shock, hopping about on his good leg, grabbing instinctively for his injured foot. Some of the men who had gathered laughed at his antics and then Grant stepped in, grabbed him by the shoulder and spun him about so that Chick faced away from him. Then he took hold of the man's belt and the back of his neck and ran him straight for the horsetrough. Townsmen scattered and Chick roared as he realized what was about to happen, but it did no good.

Grant lifted him bodily and slammed him down into the scummy water, holding the man's head under as he thrashed and bubbled and fought. He yanked him up and as Chick retched and gasped, fisted up his shirt front and leaned down to glare into the man's dripping, contorted face.

'I dunno what you're playing at, Chick, but I hope you've cooled off now.' He slapped the man lightly but stingingly across the face and thrust him back so that he sat in the trough.

The crowd roared with laughter and

Grant, breathing quite normally despite his exertions, flicked water from his shirtfront and smiled as he turned and walked back to where his package lay on the edge of the boardwalk. He stooped to pick it up and then someone yelled a warning.

Mildly surprised, Grant spun as he straightened but Chick was moving faster than he thought and the big fist drove at his jaw. He yanked his head aside but knobbly knuckles grazed his jaw and he stumbled, hitting his head on the awning post. His hat fell in the dust, revealing his long brown hair, and he clawed at the weathered wood as he went down to one knee.

Next instant, a boot smashed into his fingers where they curled about the post and he grunted in pain, saw the boot coming at him again, only this time it was aimed at his head.

He dodged and Chick grunted as the boot slammed against the post, bringing down a cloud of dust from the awning's shingles, and the jar ran up into his hip. Chick grabbed at his upper leg and grimaced as he limped back. Then Grant was on him, lifting a knee into his face, hammering at him with both fists.

Chick rolled with a couple of the blows, but two hard ones snapped his head back on his neck and his arms flailed as he tried to keep his balance. He fell to the dust but rolled away and stumbled to his feet, scooping a handful of gravel into Grant's face as the man closed in. Grant jerked his head back and Chick drove a shoulder into his chest, staggering him. He followed swiftly, launching a barrage of body blows, grunting with the effort behind each one. Grant was driven back, caught his heel in a pothole, fell.

Chick leapt at him, boots driving into his side. The crowd roared and jostled for better positions so as to see what was escalating into a much harder brawl than any of them had hoped for. Grant caught one boot in both hands, rose to his knees and swung the hopping Chick's leg aside violently. The big man flailed and stumbled to one knee. Then a mule kicked him in the middle of the face and his nose crunched and warm blood flooded down his throat as he went over backwards, seeing the sky reel above him, then darken. Another jolting blow shook him before he hit the ground. Then the street itself jarred his aching bones and he rolled on to his stomach, hawking blood and spittle, coughing.

Steel fingers twisted in his newly pomaded hair and Grant's grip slipped some. But his down-driving fist split the skin under Chick's right eye, skidded across to slam into the already battered nose. Chick slid sideways. Grant straightened, sucking in deep breaths, thinking that ought to take care of it.

In most cases it would have – *should* have – but Chick was tough and it was pure instinct that drove him up to his feet and sent him staggering back towards Grant, punching wildly.

Grant jerked his head aside, let the first

blow slip past his ear. He weaved back to avoid the second blow, but it took him under the arch of his ribs and he thought his insides were coming out of his mouth as his legs buckled.

*Man!* That was one savage blow and he was momentarily paralysed so that while he saw the knuckles zooming towards his face there was nothing he could do to avoid them.

They hit him like an express train and suddenly it was the Fourth of July as he fell forward with a shrill whistling filling his head. He slammed into the street and, head still ringing, distorting all sound, he had blurred glimpses of boots coming at him seemingly from all directions. His body jerked as they landed and he tried to fend them off feebly with his arms. His left arm was kicked up over his head so violently he thought the bone must be broken. Then the pain started in his midriff and chest and throat and he knew he was past the paralysis and he could breathe again ... even though it was bringing him back to a world filled with agony.

He took one more boot on his hip, then swept his left leg around and back in a violent arc. He felt it jar against Chick's shin and the man howled, stumbled away, cursing with the sheer pain of it.

Grant wasn't quite sure where he was or what he was seeing – everything was distorted and blurred – but he had tunnel vision so that he could focus a pale yellow circle on Chick who was getting over the shocking pain of his shin and preparing to attack again.

Grant put all he had left into a charge, catching Chick by surprise. He got a shoulder into the man's midriff, gripped him about the hips and roared like a bull buffalo as he straightened and ran at the awning post, men scattering out of the way

The weathered timber cracked, then broke under the impact of Chick's body and that corner of the awning sagged drunkenly. But Grant's aching legs drove forward and on and slammed Chick against the wall of the barbershop so violently that bottles of pomade and bay rum on shelves inside tumbled to the floor, some shattering.

Chick sagged and Grant pinned him against the clapboards with one hand around his throat and hammered his right fist into the man's bloody face again and again as if he were driving nails into hardwood.

Blood sprayed and gristle crunched, lips smashed and some of Chick's strong white teeth broke off at the gumline.

Men moved in, fighting down Grant's flailing arm, surprised at the strength in it after the punishment that the bronc-buster had taken. They prised his other hand free of Chick's throat and the battered man collapsed in a tom and bloody heap across the boardwalk, retching, gagging.

Grant's legs almost gave way, but the townsmen supported him and someone handed him a neckerchief and he wiped blood and sweat out of his eyes. They eased him down on the shop stoop and the little barber himself brought him a flat bottle of whiskey and offered it to him.

'It was worth a few busted bottles and a broken awnin' to see a fight like that!' he opined, and others in the crowd agreed. 'Who is he? Old enemy...?'

Grant drank, grimacing as the liquor stung his cut mouth, shook his head. 'Never seen ... him before,' he gasped and there was surprise amongst the onlookers.

Then Sheriff Fergus Perry pushed through, a big-bellied man of medium height with a moon face and the beginnings of a turkey neck. He thumbed back his hat above his thick eyebrows, placed both hands on his ample hips.

'You are one helluva mess, Bronco...' Then some men moved and he glimpsed the bloody, unconscious form of Chick sprawled against the wall. 'Christ! And you're the *winner!*' The sheriff shook his head slowly. 'Well, who started it and what was it about?'

Grant took another long pull at the whiskey and the barber suddenly snatched the bottle back, frowning as he examined the low level remaining.

'Fergus, I just dunno. That ranny prodded me until I got mad enough to dunk him in the horse trough. Then he went plumb loco.'

Perry frowned. 'You sayin' you don't know him?'

Grant shook his head slowly.

'Well, if he's a trouble-hunter, he's found a heap of it – and if he wants more, I'll oblige. Coupla you men get him up and drag him down to the jail house. And, Bronco, you best get that face seen to. You weren't real handsome before, but I reckon your looks might've been changed permanent after this.'

Grant wouldn't be surprised if the lawman was right.

But, a couple of hours later, as he was making his way back to the barber's to pick up his package, he was surprised to see Chick forking a fine-looking chestnut down

33

Main towards him.

Stiff, aching, breathing painfully, Grant paused, dropping a hand close to the butt of his sixgun on his right hip. Chick's face was mostly bandages and tape but he stopped the horse, folded split-knuckled hands on his saddlehorn. He shook his head at Grant.

'Relax,' he said, voice muffled. 'I don't want no more trouble with you, Brimstone man.' He was almost cheerful.

'Thought the sheriff was locking you up?' Grant said, puzzled by the man's tone. He'd had one helluva beating...

Chick shrugged. 'Said I could go if I got outta town right away. Well, nothin' to keep me here now. I done what I came for.' He looked suddenly sly. '*And* got paid for it.'

Grant frowned as the man started to knee the chestnut around him. 'Wait up. What the hell's that mean? "You done what you came for"? All I seen you do since you came to town was get a haircut and shave and try to kick my lungs out.'

Chick's smashed mouth was just visible

under the swathe of bandages. 'There you are then,' he said, as the battered lips moved in a faint smile and he started the chestnut walking past Grant. 'You're one tough *hombre*, mister.'

The bronco buster turned slowly to look after Chick as he headed towards the edge of town.

'I don't know you!' Grant called.

Chick didn't turn, merely shook his head, lifted a hand and rode slowly on.

Grant turned as Sheriff Perry came up beside him.

'Now what in hell you s'pose he meant? Did he come to Brimstone for a haircut and shave or just to fight with you?'

## 2

## Hunters

A couple of weeks later almost all signs of the fight with the mysterious 'Chick' had faded from Bronco Grant's face.

He had endured a heap of sarcasm from Dog after his return from Brimstone that day.

'Thought we not hunt mustangs till end of month?' the wiry Apache said, deadpan, his broad, dark face giving no hint that there might be any humour behind his words. At Grant's cold return look, he added, 'How come you been throw into tree then? You hurt tree?'

'Only my face, you damn heathen,' growled Grant, in that bantering, insulting tone they adopted with each other on occasion. Perversely, it was when they felt closest in their long friendship. 'And the tree was wearing a hat.'

Dog sighed. 'Ride hoss, too?'

'Yeah! He rode out of town, a lot more cheerful than I felt.'

Dog paused. 'You lose?'

'No, goddamnit! I *won!* But that son of a bitch seemed almost *happy* when he left town, couldn't even see properly for the bandages covering his face but he was *happy!*'

'Well, always think white men are loco.'

Grant grinned, despite his battered mouth. 'Ah, Dog! You're too good for me today – I give up.' And he told the Apache about Chick and the man's strange behaviour after deliberately starting the fight. 'He came at me like a runaway bull buffalo, Dog. No quarter asked or given. Then he shows up all bandaged and bruised and damn near whistling a tune he was so blamed pleased with himself. No grudges, neither.'

'What this Chick say?'

'Oh, something about doing what he came to Brimstone for. But there were just two things he did: never even had a drink in the saloon, I found out later. What he did was have a haircut and shave ... and pick a fight with me.'

Dog's dark thoughtful eyes fixed on Grant's battered features. After a long silence, he said, 'Mebbe test you.' At Grant's blank look, he added, 'See how good you fight.'

Grant's frown deepened. 'The hell for? I've never seen him in my life. And there was no grudge behind it, just a willingness, almost an impatience to get started.'

Dog nodded sagely. 'Test you, all right.'

Grant spread his hands. 'Why?'

Dog shrugged. 'Mebbe learn later.'

'What?'

'Chick must tell how tough you are first.'

'Tell who...?'

Dog shrugged.

'Ah, this is fantasy, Dog. My guess is he's

just a cowpoke who fancies himself as a brawler and somehow he found out I had a reputation as a bit of a scrapper in these parts. Mebbe he learned it from someone who was in the army with me ... yeah, could've. Lot of those boys took to trail driving and Chick had the look of a trail man. Yeah, I'd say he met someone who knew me in the army and during some camp-fire talk he mentioned how I was un-official champ of the Missouri Eighth Volunteers and Chick came and looked me up.'

Dog stared a while, shook his head once. 'That *your* fantasy, Bronco.'

They worked long and hard making up the harness and two new saddles, using the metal findings Grant had picked up in town and hides that Dog had tanned in oak bark and made supple with deer fat. They also made panniers for pack-saddles.

A "Grant" bridle or cinch was much sought-after well beyond the Brimstones, the high reputation of the workmanship and strength talked about by men who spent their working lives in the saddle. Grant sat with the springwood clamp anchored under his thighs on a tree-stump stool in the warm Fall sunlight while he laboriously saddle-stitched the leather with waxed thread. Dog sewed too but was slower and not as neat. He excelled in tanning and dyeing and dressing the finished product.

By the end of the second week they had a pile of harness and the two saddles were receiving their several coats of neatsfoot oil when Harry Best from the neighbouring Box B delivered the letter given him by McGruder who owned the general store and had a post office agency.

It was a booking from a couple of hunters who had been given Grant's name by a man called O'Grady. Grant had guided O'Grady into the Brimstones last year in search of bighorn sheep and deer. Grant had not only found the animals for O'Grady, but they had run into a bear on the trek out of the hills and Grant had seen to it that his customer got a clear shot and by now the skin would be a rug on the floor of O'Grady's den back in Chicago.

Grant ran the hunting guide business as a sideline when things were slow in the horse-ranching trade – like now. A couple of hunters booking for a two-week trek as these two wanted according to their letter, were very welcome indeed.

'We got us a couple of hunters, Dog – Bighorn, deer *and cougar!* With any stray old bears we come across thrown in! Hey, this one could see us through the winter if we have some luck with the game!'

Dog seemed unimpressed.

Grant scanned the letter again swiftly. 'Lewis and Barnett from Wichita, Kansas.'

Dog grunted.

'That's no way to greet good prospects like these gents... Barnett, who wrote the letter, says they're in the freight business. We might earn ourselves a nice leetle bonus if we find 'em what they want, Dog.'

'They kill off buffalo, now they come look

41

for bighorns and bear. White men waste meat too much.'

Grant said nothing. He savvied the Indian's point of view: it was the whites who had decimated the herds of millions of buffalo. Now the "sportsmen" who could afford it traipsed all over the country, hiring guides like Grant to lead them to other big game that they could add to their tally, or display in their homes. Indians, meantime, were half-starving on reservations where the government had placed them, denied the right to go hunting meat to supplement their rations, and white hunters left carcasses to rot while merely taking a bear's skin or a deer's antlers. Dog, once an army scout, had been lucky enough because of that to be given permission to stay with Grant after he resigned from the cavalry, but he had kin on the reservations. He also had kin hiding out with Geronimo...

'I'll write back tonight and tell 'em to come next week if they can make it,' Grant said, waving the letter. 'Don't want to leave it too long in case there's early snow in the Brimstones.'

Dog grunted again and Grant looked at him sharply before smiling faintly. 'If you think your tagging along might start up the Indian Wars again, you'd best stay here, Dog, finish them corrals and reshingle the barn roof.'

Dog grunted one more time. 'You go to white man's hell, *caballero*.' Like most Apaches, Dog spoke Spanish fluently.

Grant grinned: he'd known all along that despite his grouching, Dog would come on the hunt. That Apache blood still sang in his veins when he looked at the distant Brimstones, his old hunting ground. He took every opportunity to go there.

But his remark about Grant "going to the white man's hell" was to prove prophetic...

The train due that week was a nine-car freight but there was a single passenger car squeezed in ahead of the yellow-painted caboose.

Grant straightened from leaning against the post in the shade of the depot's single awning, took one last drag on his cheroot and flicked it down to the track where it burst in a shower of sparks amongst the cinders packed between the ties. The loco spewed black smoke that stained the sky for a quarter of a mile as it laboured up the last grade, rolled over the top and eased down to Brimstone siding.

There were only a few folk at the siding, mostly workmen waiting to unload the freight from the box cars and tarp-covered wagons. Sheriff Fergus Perry came strolling along and nodded to Grant.

'Pickin' up freight?' the lawman asked casually. When Grant glanced down at him, he added, 'See you come in earlier drivin' your buckboard.'

'Got a couple of hunters due,' Grant said shortly.

Perry nodded, not fazed by Grant's curtness. The lawman had a reputation for poking his nose into everyone's business and his hide was thick enough to handle the snubs he usually earned.

'Old customers?'

'New.'

Perry nodded. 'Mite late in the season.'

'They're businessmen. Have to grab what time they can when it's there, I guess.'

Perry nodded towards the dirty red passenger car. 'I'd say that's them.' He squinted as two well-dressed men in polished halfboots stepped down, lugging leather-trimmed canvas valises and bedrolls. They looked at ease, or maybe a mite on the superior side, Grant thought as he approached and saw the way the leaner, taller of the two was looking about him. His hands were on his hips, his high-crowned, curl-brim hat thumbed back revealing string-coloured, sweat-damp hair on a high forehead. Hard eyes swept the siding and the town beyond, his chiselled features showing a trace of contempt.

The other man was heavier, a head shorter than his companion, and he lit a cigar now, scraping the vesta on the seat of his corduroy trousers. They were sand-coloured and good quality, evident even from several yards away. His face was fleshier than the other man's but tanned and although he looked a mite overweight, Grant had a notion there was a lot of steel-hard muscle under that outer layer of fat.

Grant nodded as they turned their gazes to him.

'Mr Lewis and Mr Barnett...? I'm Bronco Grant.'

The lean one with the hard eyes had a thin mouth and it kind of stretched out a little now, not in a smile but with that touch of contempt Grant had noted when the man had studied the town.

The heavy-set man said, 'I'm Rafe Barnett.' He thrust out his hand and Grant gripped, feeling the strength in the man, knowing he had been right about the muscle beneath the layer of fat. 'This here's Harvey Lewis, my associate.'

Lewis didn't offer his hand, nodded curtly

to Grant. 'Not much of a town. Fact, it looks a dump.'

Grant smiled thinly. 'We won't waste any time in getting out then.' He lifted the valises, one in each hand, nodding his head towards his parked buckboard. 'You gents make yourselves comfortable in the shade while I load up – or would you like a drink first? Second building past the siding is a saloon...'

'Let's get moving out to your place,' Barnett said. 'Our gear's in boxcar five.' He handed Grant the freight slip and in about twenty minutes they were ready to go.

Sheriff Perry came across, smiling, thumbing back his hat, looking at the men on the seat of the buckboard.

'Welcome to Brimstone, gents. What you huntin' so late in the season?'

Grant introduced the hunters to the lawman and Barnett said, equably, 'Just about anything Mr Grant can put us on to. We'd prefer bighorn sheep, cougar and bear, but we'll settle for a set of antlers with record points.'

'You go in for all that big-game palaver then?' Perry said, and Grant saw Lewis's eyes close down and Barnett stiffened a little.

'We'll get moving, Fergus,' he said quickly, lifting the reins and setting the team forward. 'Might be some rain in that big cloud...'

Perry turned to look at the heavy, dark cloud Grant indicated and said, 'Aw, hell, we won't get none of that... It's—'

But when he turned back he found he was talking to the empty space where the buckboard had been standing.

'Coupla tough customers,' he opined half aloud, as Grant drove the men across the wooden bridge spanning Sulphur Creek and headed out towards his distant ranch.

'It's kind of spartan, gents,' Grant said apologetically, showing the hunters to their rooms at the back of the low, sprawling house. 'Was built by a man for his family but the woman and two of his boys died of cholera on the way out here and he turned back. I was able to buy cheap.'

'Yeah, looks cheap, all right,' opined Lewis, staring around the room which contained the basic furniture of bed, chair and table, and a screened-off corner for hanging clothes.

'I've a cabin in the hills we'll use as a base,' Grant told them, 'but we can camp out if you want – just that it's getting mighty cold in the hills after the sun goes down now.'

'We'll play it by ear,' Barnett said easily. 'If we're on a good game trail, don't see the sense in going all the way back to camp and having to cover the same ground next day again before we can really get started.'

'Fine. Now, would you gents care for some mighty fine sippin' whiskey before supper? Dog ought to have it ready in about five minutes by the smell of it.'

A mouth-watering odour of savoury stew filled the house. Lewis's shoulders stiffened and he glanced over his shoulder as he started to unstrap his bedroll.

'Dog?'

'Running Dog – he's my Indian tracker. Been with me since my cavalry days and–'

'Lose him,' Lewis said curtly, cutting off Grant.

The horse rancher blinked. 'What?'

'Lose the Injun. We don't need him along.'

Grant felt himself tightening up and flicked his grey gaze from one man to the other. Barnett's face seemed blanker than Lewis's but he made no comment so Grant was forced to conclude he backed his companion's words.

'I always take Dog on the hunt,' Grant said, keeping his voice steady. 'He's the best tracker in the country. That's why all my clients go away satisfied. You want a particular type of game and Dog'll find it for you.'

'Get rid of him. We booked this on *your* reputation, not any Injun's.'

Barnett still hadn't spoken and Grant looked from one man to the other. 'You gents got something against Indians?'

'Yeah, we have,' Lewis said instantly, and he faced Grant with a barely restrained aggression. 'Why don't matter to you – we're payin', and we're tellin' you to get rid of this Injun.'

Grant held the man's cold gaze a moment, slid his eyes to Barnett. 'That the way you want it, too?'

Barnett pursed his lips, flicked his eyes to Lewis and then back to Grant. 'Generally I go along with Harve – but you seem to think this Dog is kinda special. How come?'

Grant squared-up to them, his face as hard and neutral as he could make it. 'Giving you back your words, Mr Lewis, why don't matter. He's my tracker and he's part of the deal.'

Lewis leaned forward some. 'Mister, there *ain't* no deal if you bring that Injun along!'

Grant held his sober look but his mind was racing. He needed the money these two would spend. They'd already paid a deposit, but...

'Half your deposit's refundable, gents, but before you jump in and grab it, think about this: if you're serious about this hunt, and I figure you must be to come all this way with so much gear, then you won't find bigger-point antlers anywhere else, nor longer curves on a sheep's horns. There're cougars in there near tall as a mustang pony and I've personally seen a bear nearly nine feet high when he rears up. Now, I'm not saying I can guarantee you'd get any of this game, but I am saying that you'll have the best chance possible with Dog doing the tracking. He grew up in the Brimstones.'

Lewis stiffened even more and his face whitened, knobs of muscle standing out along his jawline. 'He's a goddamn *Apache* as well?'

Grant nodded. Lewis swore, rounding on Barnett. 'That does it, Rafe! Wonder I didn't smell the varmint soon's I come in here!'

While he had been speaking, he had dropped his hand to his sixgun butt. Grant stepped between the men, side-on so he could still watch Barnett.

'Don't draw that!' he snapped at Lewis, and the man looked a mite surprised when he realized he was gripping his gun butt. 'You got a hate-on for Apaches, best thing you can do is go back where you come from. I'll drive you into town but you'll have to wait a week for the train.'

Lewis curled a lip. His nostrils flared, but he seemed stuck for words, looked swiftly at Barnett. The man was just lighting a cigar.

'Mr Grant, Harve's sister and mother were taken by Apaches. He was the one found what was left of 'em. Took him three years to track down the particular bunch. Happened in Arizona some time back. You can't blame Harve for being prejudiced.'

Lewis was shaking now, his face gaunt and sunken, eyes seeming to stand out of his head.

Grant nodded slowly. 'They are a savage people,' he said quietly. 'I've seen their work, and I'm sorry for what happened to your kinfolk, Mr Lewis, but Dog wasn't one of the band that did it. He served in the army with me for four years and before that lived in New Mexico ... and he's still the best tracker. If there's anything you really want in the Brimstones, Dog'll find it for you.'

The hunters exchanged a look that puzzled Grant: he couldn't read it at all. Barnett studied the burning end of his cigar.

'We understood it was you who knew the Brimstones better than anyone else.'

Grant shrugged. 'Better'n any white man, but I couldn't find my way out of a root cellar compared to Dog in those hills.'

Lewis seemed calmer, but only because of a series of unreadable looks from Barnett, who was quickly emerging as the dominant character of the two. Lewis scowled at Grant.

'Just keep that red bastard away from me.'

The smell of the Mulligan was suddenly stronger and they all turned as Dog, holding a big iron kettle in one hand, plates in the other, announced from the doorway, flatly, 'Stew ready.'

He stepped towards the big scarred dining-table passing close to Lewis who moved back quickly, hand dropping to his gun butt again. Dog gave him a contemptuous look and set the steaming kettle on the table and began placing the plates, his back turned to the hunter.

'They tell me you're a pretty good tracker, Dog?' Lewis said tightly.

'Yes.' Dog didn't turn around, began ladling out the stew.

'Where'd you get a name like "Dog", anyways? Hey! And when I speak to you, you look at me, OK?'

Lewis grabbed Dog's shoulder and spun him quickly. The Indian had a ladleful of stew in his hand and it came around and spilled all down the front of Lewis's shirt and jacket. The man swore and leapt back, hand slapping his gun butt – there was no doubt he was going to draw this time.

Then he froze, staring with disbelief as he found Grant's sixgun cocked and rock-steady in his fist, the muzzle bare inches from his nose.

'I told you not to try and draw that gun,' Grant said quietly.

Lewis's breath hissed out between his teeth and he slowly unclasped his fingers from around his gun butt. 'You had that Colt in your hand all along!' he accused, but Grant shook his head slightly.

'I was wearing it ... in the holster. You're just not as fast as you thought, Mr Lewis.'

Lewis scowled. 'That damn Injun dumped that stew on me a'purpose!'

'Didn't look that way to me,' Grant said mildly, arching eyebrows quizzically at Running Dog. The Apache shrugged.

His flat stare held Lewis's hostile one without a hint of apology and Lewis flushed, knowing there would be none forthcoming. He glared at Barnett and Grant frowned as the other man nodded very slightly, but enough to tighten Lewis's lips.

It was some kind of signal and Barnett

said carefully, 'Let it go, Harve. It was an accident... Now, get yourself cleaned up and have some of this mighty fine-smelling stew before it gets cold.'

Lewis took out a kerchief and began brushing the stew off his jacket and trousers. Dog finished serving and started for the kitchen door.

'Dog, you eat with us as usual,' Grant said sharply, but the Indian kept on going out of the room.

'Got chores to do.'

Grant turned slowly back to his plate of stew under the hard gazes of the hunters. He felt uncomfortable.

Almost as if he was being put to – or had just come through – some sort of test.

This was going to be a mighty interesting trip into the Brimstones, he allowed silently. Mighty damn interesting.

# 3

## Trek

The pack mules were strung out, labouring under panniers stuffed tight with the gear brought along by Barnett and Lewis. There were a couple of light wooden boxes, too, fastened to one mule, but the hunters had avoided answering when Grant had asked what they contained.

All in all, there were five mules, three more than Grant usually took into the Brimstones when he was leading a hunting expedition. And there were a few odd things about these two and he figured to stay alert.

Some old hunch from the fighting days warned him not to take everything at face value with Lewis and Barnett.

Dog rode ahead most times, scouting the

trail, setting-up camp and starting the supper. They ate cold during the day. Lewis had chosen to ignore him mostly but there had been once or twice when the man had made rough remarks. Running Dog, like most Apaches, had learned long ago not to react to the baiting of white men and his face was blank, as if chiselled from granite, as he went about his chores.

They stopped in a draw with a collapsed cutbank at one end and Grant pointed. 'That loose earth'll make a good backstop for bullets if you gents'd like to sight-in your rifles.'

They seemed a mite surprised, Grant thought, but Barnett recovered first and said, 'Sure, why not?'

They had their guns in padded canvas cases and Grant watched as Barnett took a long leather cylinder from his gun case after removing the oiled rifle, a Remington bolt-action in .30 calibre.

He took a long copper tube and some clamps from the cylinder and clipped the tube on top of the rifle. He smiled crookedly at Grant.

'Best German optics money can buy. Got cross hairs etched into the lens and a range scale worked by this here knurled knob. Get me within half a mile of the game and he's as good as dead.'

Grant pursed his lips. 'Most hunters I bring in here like to get a helluva lot closer than that before shooting.'

Barnett arched his eyebrows. 'That so? Well, this saves a lot of stalking and there's less chance of spooking the target.'

'Thought you gents were sportsmen.' They looked at Grant as he added flatly, 'You don't give the game much of a sporting chance with a 'scope like that.'

'Aim is to bring in the trophy, right?' Barnett said shortly. Then he smiled thinly, patted his slight paunch. 'A mite outa condition to be bellying-up for mile after mile just to see if I can stalk a deer or a sheep without spooking him. All I want to do is shoot the son of a bitch.'

'Anyways,' Lewis said, giving Grant a hard look. 'How close you want to get to a bear or a cougar?'

'Usually a lot closer than you'll be getting I guess,' Grant said, and swung down. 'I'll set up some targets on a measured range.'

He strode forward, counting his steps, dropping a marker at fifty, a hundred and two hundred yards. Barnett produced some square cardboard targets with bullseyes and Dog and Grant set them up.

'Damn long-range hunters!' Grant murmured, as they moved up the draw. 'There's not so much game left in these hills that they can shoot from one ridge to the other to bring it down.'

'Tote in armchair next,' was Dog's way of agreeing.

But they were beautiful weapons the hunters were using. They had a selection of calibres and actions, bolt and lever, and each had a top grade shotgun, over-and-under, British made. Lewis showed Grant a box of brass shells for this weapon, with just the tip of a huge lead projectile, heavily ribbed in spirals showing.

'Slugs. Use 'em in the shotgun which is a smoothbore, that ribbing gives 'em a twist and a flatter trajectory. You ain't seen the bear that'll walk away with a couple of them in his brisket.'

'All right for bear, but they'd blow a deer apart. Or a sheep.'

Lewis smiled. 'Ought to see what they can do to a cougar! And a woodchuck! *Man!*'

Grant was liking these two less and less...

They were good shots, with or without the aid of the telescopic sight, placing the bullets from the hand-loaded cartridges right where they wanted. Barnett would nominate a segment of the target and proceed to put five shots almost through the same hole in that area. Lewis wasn't quite that good, but he was good enough.

Before they moved on, he fixed a 'scope to his drop-breech Creedmoor, settled behind a low rock and scanned the timbered slopes above the draw. He motioned to Grant.

'Look through the field glasses at that stand of piñon. The big one with the bark rubbed through by deer antlers ... got it? Look to the left, couple yards. See that woodchuck scratching away at the layer of needles?'

Grant focused as Lewis turned back to his weapon, sighted briefly and then fired. The sharp crack, entirely different to the flat booming sound of a Winchester, slapped at Grant's ears and he jerked slightly as the tiny woodchuck he was looking at suddenly disintegrated in a shower of fur and blood and flying guts.

'Christ!' he exclaimed, lowering the glasses, snapping his gaze down to where Lewis was stretched out, grinning, the breech smoking as he dropped it open and caught the hot brass case for later reloading. 'Way too much gun, Lewis!'

'Wouldn't get much of a stew outa him! What distance you say that was? Seven hundred yards? Seven-fifty?'

Grant simply walked away. He didn't trust

himself to speak. Not that he had any particular affection for woodchucks, but it was the act itself that disgusted him. And the fact that Lewis had so obviously enjoyed blowing that small animal apart from such a distance.

'Let's get going, Dog,' he called to the Indian, who was watching from atop a boulder, silent and deadpan.

Lewis was chuckling, in a good mood, as he and Barnett cleaned their weapons before putting them away.

'You wanna try the Creedmoor before I put it back in the case, Grant?' Lewis asked, kind of taunting.

'Only if you go stand by that piñon.'

Lewis's grin faded slowly, but he nodded. 'Yeah, I think you'd like using me as a target, all right.'

'Quit talking rubbish!' snapped Barnett. 'Let's go. We've a long ways to travel yet.'

Grant wondered why Barnett thought so. True, he hadn't given any indication which part of the Brimstones they would be hunting, but the way Barnett spoke, it sounded as if he knew exactly where he was going...

Three days later, each man had bagged a stag which Dog and Grant had skinned-out and caped, leaving the hides and heads on an ants' nest for cleaning. They ate venison at every meal for the next couple of days when he took them climbing up the steep, rocky slopes in search of bighorn sheep. Dog scouted ahead, brought back dung in various stages of drying-out, but none was fresh. Then two sheep were spotted on the next ridge over, sizing each other up, obviously getting ready to fight when the massive bosses of the curling horns would crash together like a shotgun blast, echoing through the ranges.

Barnett snatched his gun case from Grant immediately and settled down to use the Remington with the 'scope.

'Rather you got on that other ridge to make your shot, Mr Barnett,' Grant told him tightly. 'Make sure of your kill.'

'You would, huh?' Barnett went on settling himself, the fore end of the rifle resting in a padded forked support which he drove into the ground. 'Well, you don't happen to be doing the shooting.'

Grant kicked the rest away from under the gun and Barnett swore, rolled on to his side and then jumped to his feet.

'You son of a bitch! Look at the scratches you've put on my gun's fore end!'

'You're a fine shot, Barnett,' Grant told him steadily. 'Don't be plumb lazy. Do a little stalking. You'll be surer of getting your game. I won't allow you to shoot from this far off. The game doesn't have much chance at all.'

Grant stiffened as a gun muzzle pressed against his spine. Lewis spoke close to his ear. 'You do what *we* want, mister. We're the ones paying for this hunt.'

Grant spun so fast that later Lewis wasn't too sure just what had happened. But suddenly his gun arm was jarred and he staggered and then a fist smashed against his jaw, another taking him in the ribs. He fell back against a rock, dazed, tasting blood. Grant had his own sixgun out now, cocked, covering both men. Dog rose silently from behind a rock, startling Barnett he was so close, a Bowie knife with a well-honed blade glinting in his hand.

Barnett took a deep breath, lifted both hands. 'All right, all *right!* You must lose a few customers this way, Grant!'

Grant shook his head. 'You're the first long-distance shooters I've struck, except for buffalo hunters who hardly count. We'll break camp and we can be back at the foot of the mountain by nightfall. We'll start back for my place at sun-up.'

Lewis was rubbing his jaw, glaring his undisguised hatred at Grant. Barnett frowned, looking surprised.

'You want to turn back?'

Grant held the man's gaze a long, silent moment. 'Don't you? I mean, you've lost those sheep, they're long gone, and I don't aim to let you do any long-range shooting: in my camp, a good hunter earns his shot.'

Barnett shrugged, watching the tight-faced Lewis closely. 'You make the rules. It's your territory, after all. Like I said earlier, I'm a mite out of condition. I've been ill for some time and this is sort of part of my recuperation, but if you insist we stalk close to game from here on in, I guess that's the way it'll have to be.' He looked towards Lewis. 'Right, Harve?'

Lewis scowled and stooped and carefully picked up his gun and dropped it back in its holster. He stepped close to Grant.

'You're lucky we need you, Grant! But there'll come a day when we don't - we'll settle things then.'

There was murder in his narrowed eyes.

'Look forward to it, Lewis,' Grant said easily – but he wondered why the sudden backdown.

Barnett had stepped away smartly when Grant had mentioned terminating the hunt. And Lewis, busting to kill Grant, had said clearly that they still needed him.

They weren't that keen on hunting, he reckoned, so what the hell did Lewis mean?

The puzzle kept him awake for some time after he slid into his bedroll when supper was over. The hunters tossed and turned and murmured between themselves on their side of the fire. He didn't hear a sound from Dog, but that was normal. You never knew when Dog was sleeping or prowling the night, looking for danger.

For this was Indian country, crawling in parts with wild Apaches and renegades who refused to go under the government's net and live on a reservation. Over the years, Grant had had little trouble with them, but there was always the chance some time, drunk on *tiswin* or just feeling plain ornery, when they would hit one of his parties.

He was drifting off when he felt a small weight on his upper left arm. He knew it was Dog's hand. The weight disappeared and after a minute, Grant slid out of his bedroll and in stockinged feet and holding his sixgun, moved up-slope, away from the hunters across the banked coals of the fire.

Dog was crouched beside a boulder and Grant moved in close. 'What?'

Dog hissed his words. 'They talk. I hear. They mention "Chick".'

Grant stiffened, involuntarily touched the fresh scar above his eye. 'What'd they say?'

'Chick tell them you *very* tough – and know Brimstones.'

'The hell's going on, Dog? Seems you could've been right when you said Chick was testing me. I've had the same notion about Lewis and Barnett: seeing what I can do.'

'Watch Lewis, Bronco. He hardly touch his supper. He feeding on his hate – for you. He gonna kill you first chance he get.'

Grant nodded, jaw firming.

'But not yet,' Dog added. 'They still trying you out.'

Grant shook his head slowly. 'Beats the hell outa me, Dog. What do they want from me?'

70

Neither man had the answer, but Grant thought for a time the next day at their nooning on a hillside under the shade of some trees that he was going to find out.

Dog was away into the hills, scouting for the tracks of a large cougar they had been following through the high country all morning. Lewis sat with his back against a boulder, smoking, looking surly as usual.

Barnett was studying an ordnance survey map of the Brimstones and making notes. He had done so on other occasions, too, said he was keeping a journal and aimed to write some articles for hunting magazines when he got back home.

Grant was preparing the sandwiches of cold venison on the last of the bread Dog had baked Indian-fashion a couple of days ago.

'Bronco,' called Barnett: he had taken to using Grant's nickname now and had, in fact, been going out of his way to be friendly since the blow-up over the long-range shooting. 'Got a minute?'

Grant strolled across and squatted beside Barnett. He saw now that the man not only had a copy of the official map of the area, but also a smaller, hand-drawn map on a crumpled piece of paper. He carefully folded it before Grant had time to see more than a few pencilled lines. The hunter looked at the guide.

'I make it we're about here on the big map ... that right?'

Grant saw that the man had been marking in their trail every day and his latest cross-within-a-circle was pretty close to the canyon where they were now.

'Yeah, that's about right.'

Barnett nodded, looked sideways and up into Grant's face. 'You ever hear of a place called Sabre Peak?'

Grant fought to keep his face straight and not too interested. 'Heard of it, yeah.' He swept an arm about in a vague arc. 'Lies in that direction, way to the south-west, according to what I've heard.'

'You've never been there or seen it?'

Barnett's voice was sharp now and out of the corner of his eye, Grant saw Lewis heave to his feet and amble across. 'Saw it once in the distance – leastways, feller I was with said it was Sabre Peak. I haven't been that far south: all the game I want seems to be around this neck of the woods.'

'That so?' Barnett said. 'Well, we'd like to go that way ... can do?'

Grant hesitated briefly. 'Can be done, all right, but like I said, there's not much game down there. Someone tell you there was?'

'Guess I must've heard it some place,' Barnett allowed. 'Cougars and bears, I was told.'

'Chick tell you that?' Grant asked softly, and he was aware that Lewis, behind and slightly to one side stiffened. Barnett looked at Grant blankly.

'Chick? Chick who?'

'Never did know his last name. He rode into town a few weeks back, went out of his way to pick a fight with me, then rode on out. Dog heard you talking about him last night.'

'What's that stinkin' Injun doing eavesdroppin' on us?' demanded Lewis, hand close to his gun butt again, his eyes challenging.

'Sound carries at night in these hills. Dog was just doing his job. There was no intentional eavesdropping.'

Lewis scowled but Barnett shook his head, saying, 'I don't know what he thought he heard but we weren't talking about any "Chick"–' He paused, snapped his fingers. 'Wait! Harve, you mentioned that little gal who chased you all over Dodge, I believe. Said she had a husband who was mighty tough and remember you saying "That chick from the Garter in Dodge".'

'Yeah, b'lieve you're right, Rafe,' Lewis cut in, still looking bleakly at Grant. 'Your goddamn tame dog oughta clean his ears out, Grant. An' you tell him I see him sneaking around my side of the camp again and I'll shoot first, talk afterwards.'

'You got any messages like that for Dog, you tell him yourself,' Grant snapped, turning back to Barnett. 'Now what about this Sabre Peak you want to see?'

'Don't want to see *it* in particular, but we'd like to go into that country.'

Grant gestured to the folded, hand-drawn map that Barnett still held. 'Something to do with that other map?'

'You never mind!' snapped Lewis, and Grant spun towards the man fast as he heard the whisper of a gun sliding out of leather. Lewis had his sixgun raised, ready to slam it down against Grant's head. But he never made the blow.

Something zipped down past Grant's face, clipping the outer edge of his hatbrim, whipping between him and Lewis. The hunter grunted, staggered, grabbing at his side as the arrow sliced through his jacket and across his ribs, drawing blood before it quivered in the hard ground behind him.

Grant's own pistol was in his hand now and he dived headlong towards the rock where his rifle rested, yelling, 'Get under cover!'

As he shouted the words, a dozen or more Apaches came swarming down out of the rocks, old rifles thundering, bows twanging, blood-chilling cries echoing from the walls of the canyon.

## 4

## Bad Medicine Country

Barnett and Lewis reacted swiftly, grabbing their weapons, turning to meet the attack, guns hammering as they retreated to the bigger rocks.

Grant was already crouched between two eggshaped boulders, his Winchester to his shoulder, beading leaping figures, finger easing pressure on the trigger as they dropped from sight just as he was about to fire. The army had taught him never to waste bullets and he held his fire until he caught one squarely in his sights, blasted the man in mid-air, the body spinning with flailing limbs.

Bullets ricocheted from the rock in front on him. An arrow broke just above his head, the pieces falling across his shoulders. He ducked lower, shot at another running Apache, missed, saw the man's startled leap to one side. He had tried to dive over a rock but misjudged and rolled to the ground dazed. He never rose again.

Grant levered in a fresh shell even as he searched for another target. The hunters were safely in their protective rocks now and he saw Lewis fumbling with the gleaming shotgun, thumbing two bright brass cartridges into the breech: the ones containing the massive slugs. The man brought the gun to his shoulder with practised ease and fired instantly. An Indian just lifting his head from behind a dead-fall to see the situation suddenly disappeared, a fine pink mist hanging in the air, the silver-grey log spattered with gore. That man had literally lost his head.

Barnett had his Remington going, the smoking brass of expended cartridges glittering as the ejector flung them high with the slick, oiled clash of the bolt working.

Grant saw one of Barnett's targets smashed into the side of the canyon with his left arm hanging by a shred of flesh and splintered white bone from the shoulder.

The others had gone to ground now after such a hot reception, but, glancing up to the higher walls, Grant glimpsed movement up there and figured there were reinforcements, Indians going along the rim, aiming to cut off their retreat so as to bottle them up in the canyon.

'This is a big bunch!' he called through the echoing gunfire. 'Mount up and make a break outa the canyon or we're gonna be buried here! I'll bring the mules!'

Luckily they hadn't unharnessed the pack animals or even removed the lead rope that held them together. He paused to thumb fresh shells into the hot Winchester, ducked as an arrow zipped across the boulder. He didn't bother looking for the shooter: the man would've lifted up like a jack-in-the-box, fired off the arrow and dropped back before it hit the boulder. Anyway, it was just to let him know they were still around and, also, possibly, to make him keep his head down while the others on the rim worked down to cut off the hunters' retreat.

There was no sign of Dog, but Grant wasn't worried about him. Dog could take care of himself and would help where he could.

Lewis and Barnett had reached their mounts, were pulling cinches tight, swinging up into leather. Grant tightened the cinch strap on his bay, snatched up the mule-team's rope and hit the stirrup as there came a cry from the Indians – much closer than he expected. They must have been creeping in amongst the rocks and scrub.

But they had been discovered now and there were sudden bird calls and animal sounds – signals to the ones on the rim, letting them know what was happening.

As he settled into the saddle, taking a couple of turns of the mules' rope around the horn, the Indians rose from their cover and charged in a desperate attempt to prevent the white men clearing the canyon before those up on the rim could seal it off.

The ones attacking in the canyon were afoot, leaping from rock to rock, but now that he was mounted and could see better, Grant saw that at least some on the rim were mounted, riding fast and recklessly in their attempt to trap the whites.

His guess was that this band of renegades had been watching the hunting party all along and had seen Lewis's and Barnett's fancy weapons and coveted them. They would also want the mules – mule meat was high on their menu, even above horseflesh – and the packs on the animals' backs. The whole party must look like treasure-on-the-hoof to these Apaches who lived wild, barely surviving in winter and often having to go far afield for water in the burning summers.

Lewis had reloaded his shotgun with shot-shells now and the weapon thundered twice as he rode. The charge of one barrel lay a large grey streak across some sandstone boulders, but the second charge brought a scream from a leaping Indian and he fell from sight, writhing as he clawed at a shattered leg.

Barnett had sheathed his Remington in favour of his saddle carbine and he was shooting as fast as he could work lever and trigger, knees gripping his running mount. Grant used his sixgun and was glad of the close-range weapon when suddenly an Apache launched himself with a shrill scream from a ledge to his right. Grant hauled rein hard and the bay pawed the air, wickering as it came up on to its rear legs. The manoeuvre caused the Apache to miss his dive and he hit the ground with a gasping thud but tried to roll out of it, still clasping his long-bladed knife. Grant leaned from the saddle and put a bullet into him. It wasn't a fatal wound, but the man went down and by then Grant was racing past and the Indian was forced to roll aside to avoid being trampled by the mules.

He glanced ahead and saw the men from

the rim were now on the downslope, racing for the narrow cutting that led out of the canyon. The wider exit at the far end was cut off by the line of Apaches on foot. Arrows whistled around the white men. The old wired-up guns cracked and misfired, but sent enough bullets to make them keep their heads down. Grant holstered his Colt, slid the rifle out of the long scabbard and triggered at the first three Indians making a flat-out run for the bottleneck entrance. His volley brought down one horse and rider, but the others slid over their mounts' backs, clinging to the mane on the far side, not shooting back at him, making for the entrance.

Then Lewis rode out from some trees where he had angled away from two Indians, ignored the men pursuing him, and his shotgun roared, filling the smoke-hazed canyon with its thunder. One of the racing Indians left the saddle as if jerked by a wire and his horse faltered, limped away to the side. The other Apache ran on but there wasn't much he could do alone to block the entrance. In any case, Barnett put two slugs into his back, one snapping the man's spine.

The war-whoops of the Indians had taken on an angry, frustrated sound now as the white men hit the bottleneck and thundered on through. Guns banged, arrows flew, even lances were thrown, but to no avail. The white men were breaking out...

Grant was last man through and he was almost jerked from the saddle, his horse yanked sideways and back, starting to go down. Even before he tripped in the saddle as he fought the reins he knew what had happened. One of the mules had been hit and sure enough, there was the last mule in the team, down and honking as it thrashed in the dust.

Cursing, Grant made ready to leap from leather and run back and cut the rope that attached the downed mule to the bucking, snorting mule ahead.

But suddenly a new gun boomed from the rocks, a flat, hammer-on-plank sound which he recognized as the Colt revolving rifle favoured by Running Dog.

And there was his Apache friend, riding his pinto out of the rocks, standing in stirrups, his Colt rifle banging, knocking two Apaches down, sending a third wheeling away, tangling with others following. Then Dog's mount skidded and the Indian quit leather, ran forward, slashed at the rope around the dead mule's head and dodged the kicking hoofs of the wild-eyed mule ahead in the line. Dog waved Grant on frantically even as he leapt back on to his pinto, lying low as arrows zipped over his body.

Grant got going again, Dog bringing up the rear now, dropping the used cylinder out of the Colt rifle, clicking another fully loaded one into place and turning to shoot at the attackers.

They cleared the canyon and Grant looked around for Barnett and Lewis, saw they were heading into tangled foothills of another range off to his left. They weren't sticking around to help Grant or Running Dog. They were intent only on saving their own necks. Somehow it didn't surprise him.

Grant went after them and Dog followed, emptying his rifle again, sheathing it this time because his other spare magazines were in his saddle-bags. He drew his Remington Army .44 pistol from his belt and thumbed the hammer.

The pursuit lasted well into the afternoon but by the time the shadows were starting to darken the narrow passes and draws, the Apaches were dropping back and suddenly they were gone.

One moment they were bunched, falling back slowly, next there was absolutely no sign of them, no dust hanging in the air, nothing. They'd vanished, as if swallowed by the earth.

Lewis and Barnett reined down fifty yards further on and, sweating, begrimed, panting some, they waited for Grant and Dog to catch up.

'The hell did they go?' asked Lewis,

standing in stirrups, squinting into the weltering sun.

'They decided they'd had enough, is all,' Grant said. 'Apaches tend to be like that. They figure they've fought hard and long enough, can't see an easy victory within their reach and they just quit.'

'Likely hiding amongst those hills?' asked Barnett warily, but Grant shook his head.

'No. They've quit. We're OK now.'

Lewis curled a lip in Dog's direction. 'Yeller – yeller clear through, like all Injuns.'

There was a challenge there but Dog's face gave nothing away. He busied himself reloading the cylinders for his Colt rifle. Lewis sneered, opened his mouth to speak but Grant snapped, 'Haven't you had enough fighting, Lewis?'

The man swivelled his gaze to the rancher. 'Not when I get a chance to bust a cap on yeller-bellied Injuns.'

'That's enough, Harve,' Barnett said mildly, reloading his own weapons. Then he used his rifle to point to a distant triangular peak almost lost in the late afternoon mists. 'What's that yonder, Bronco?'

Grant had already seen it and didn't look in that direction, instead kept his gaze on Barnett. 'That's Sabre Peak – we've come a long ways south of our trail during the chase.'

He watched the hunters exchange glances. Barnett scrubbed a hand around his soft-looking jaw.

'Long way from here?'

'Quite a spell of riding. Couple of ridges to cross and I'm not sure what's between.'

'Thought you was s'posed to know the Brimstones better'n anyone?' Lewis said, a growling edge to his words.

'Most of 'em, yeah – but that's kind of bad medicine country. Not even the Indians go there.'

The men looked at Dog. The Apache returned their stares silently, expression-lessly.

'It's superstition as far as whites are concerned, I guess,' Grant told them. 'But to them it's Number One bad medicine. In fact, they call it Hell's Doorway in there.'

Dog made a slight, brief hissing sound and the hunters' heads snapped around, but his face was totally unreadable. He said nothing.

But Grant hadn't missed the flare of sudden interest on Barnett's and Lewis's faces when he had mentioned "Hell's Doorway"...

There was a sudden commotion amongst the sweating, ill-tempered mules and all eyes swung towards them. The mule that had been toting one of the long wooden boxes had apparently been grazed by a bullet across the shoulder and the weight of the box had become too much for it. Now, in its pain and frustration, it tried to scrape the box off the packframe, rammed it against a boulder.

'Get that goddamn jughead!' snapped Lewis, and Barnett, too, looked both alarmed and angry.

Too late. The pine panels splintered and

then one end fell out of the coffin-like box.

Grant blinked as the contents spilled out: coil after coil of rope, blocks and tackles, harnesses and shackles. It all fell in an untidy heap beside the rock and, relieved of the weight, the mule settled down some.

But Lewis and Barnett looked ready to kill.

'You do mountain climbing, too?' Grant asked quietly, gesturing to the rope.

Lewis scowled and started forward but Barnett halted him by dropping his rifle across the man's chest.

'Hold up, Harve, it's a reasonable question.'

'Then you answer him.' Lewis sounded peeved.

Barnett nodded. 'Bronco, I told you we'd like to see the country near Sabre Peak. We're a lot closer now – you can take us, can't you? I don't mean for nothing, there'd be a couple hundred in it for you on top of the hunting fee we've already paid you.'

Grant's gaze touched Dog before he set it

on the hunters. Lewis was tense and tight-lipped, almost begging Grant to start something. Barnett looked – anxious, was the best word he could think of,

'I don't know that country very well. I told you.'

Barnett gestured to Dog. 'The Apache ... he can show us the way, can't he? You said he was raised in this country.'

Grant saw Dog stiffen in the saddle. 'You won't get Dog going in there.'

Barnett frowned. 'Superstition?'

Lewis scoffed, 'Yeller, more like it!'

'Shut up, Lewis,' Grant told the man. 'You know nothing about it. Dog's an Apache and his tribe keep right away from the country you're asking me to take you to. He's been raised on the stories of bad medicine the tribal elders tell. He believes them just the same as some white folk believe the stories in the Bible. There's nothing to scoff at and you keep it up, Lewis, you're likely to get your scalp lifted.'

'By ol' Yaller Dog there?' Lewis smiled

crookedly. 'Geez, I don't think I'm gonna be able to sleep tonight, Rafe!'

Barnett ignored the man and Dog busied himself cleaning one of the chambers in his rifle's cylinder that was fouled with un-burned black powder.

'Bronco, we won't put any pressure on Dog. Like you say, it's his religion, sort of, well – fair enough. So it comes back to you. Extra couple of hundred suit you then, Bronco?'

It did: Grant could do a lot with the extra money and it was easy enough to reach the country Barnett wanted, despite what he had told them. But Grant wondered what they were after there. There was little game and no gold or silver that he had ever heard of...

Before he could answer, Barnett said quickly, 'Fact, Dog can help us out, anyway, and earn himself a few extra bucks.'

'Now listen, Rafe!' Lewis began, face tightening, but Barnett ignored him once more, looking from Grant to the Apache.

'Thing is, there's a third member of our ... expedition, ought to be in Brimstone by now. The passenger train arrived yesterday by my calculations, that about right?'

Grant nodded. 'You never said anything in your letter about a third man.'

'He wasn't sure if he could get away, but he was gonna try and make the next train to Brimstone. Dog can go fetch him, can't he?'

'Ask him. He's his own man.'

Lewis spat as Barnett turned to the Apache who nodded and asked, 'How much?'

'Twenty – no, make it twenty-five bucks?'

'Take three days. Cost you forty dollar.'

'OK. You bring my friend to Sabre Peak in three days and one of us'll meet you. That suit you?'

'Dry wash this side Sabre Peak. Bronco meet me.'

'Sure,' Barnett agreed readily. 'Anything you say. You read?'

'Little bit only.'

Barnett took his leather-bound notebook

from his jacket pocket and wrote swiftly in it, tearing out the page and handing it to the Apache. 'Show that to the desk clerk at the Hotel Colorado. He'll tell you whether my friend's arrived. I'll just write a note I want you to mail for me, too.' He looked at Grant. 'Need to let a business associate know I'll be delayed some.'

Grant kept his face blank but he was wondering what the hell he'd gotten himself into here. Lewis and Barnett had had this planned all along – the hunt was just a blind to get them into the Brimstones. He slid his gaze to the spilled ropes still lying untidily where they had fallen from the pine box. Now, what the hell could they be after?

Yeah, something mighty queer was going on. Maybe he ought to hold out for more money. Or just ride away. *Now!*

## 5

## Devil Land

There was a delay at the first watering stop and neither Barnett nor Lewis cared much for it. They said so loudly, but there was no choice.

Grant had brought them to a series of shallow tanks, the rockholes covered with flat slabs of shale. Only one of the three tanks had any water in it and it was fouled with beetles and small, dead lizards. Grant lay full-length, used his tin coffee mug to dig out the mud in the bottom until he reached a level of coarse sand. He sat back, sweating, allowing the water to ooze slowly up. It was cloudy but it would settle clear and free of bugs eventually.

Grant looked up as the hunters came

across, Lewis carrying his shotgun, one barrel loaded with buckshot, the other with one of the massive killer slugs.

'We've come a long way south, haven't we?' Barnett asked.

Lewis looked menacing, swinging his gun towards Grant.

Grant shrugged, lighting one of his dwindling supply of cheroots. 'Thought it safer to skirt some of those washes and gulches. Can't trust the ground round here.'

'Or the goddamn guide, you ask me!' Lewis growled, but Barnett signed for him to hush up.

'What the hell does that mean? The ground?' he asked.

The guide gestured with his cheroot. 'Sinkhole country. Ground's not stable.'

'Seems all right to me,' Barnett said quietly.

'Sure. Looks and feels OK, then suddenly the earth opens up and you're on your way to hell. Fact there's supposed to be a crumbling mesa somewhere in here called

Hell's Doorway. Part of the top collapsed a long time ago and legend has it that a whole wagon train was swallowed up.'

Grant was surprised when Barnett paled a little and Lewis swore. Frowning, he flicked his gaze from one man to the other.

'What's wrong?'

Barnett recovered first but he didn't look happy. 'The thought of falling into the bowels of the earth – well, I've always been claustrophobic. Makes me shudder imagining that long, dark drop. But, whole wagon trains? Surely that's an exaggeration?'

Grant shrugged again. 'That's the talk. I told you, I don't know this country. The Indians won't come within miles of it. But at least that means we don't have to worry about being attacked.'

The hunters were silent and Grant figured it might as well be now as later, cleared his throat, and asked, 'You gents wouldn't want to tell me why you want to come into this kinda country, would you?'

'No,' Lewis said flatly, but Barnett seemed a mite uncertain, finally shook his head.

'Not necessary right now, Bronco. Perhaps later ... I hope I can trust that tame Apache of yours to do what I've paid him for.'

'One thing, he's not tame; another, he's not mine. Told you already, Dog's his own man. You might notice he's not like most Indians, doesn't slide his gaze away from a white man's face. He looks you square in the eyes. And when he says he'll do something he'll do it – whether it's lead you to water or ... kill you.'

That seemed to quieten them down and the water in the rockhole now being a few inches deep and clear, they filled the canteens, drank their fill, then let the animals in one by one. It took a deal of time, because the thirsty team drank deeply and they had to wait for more water to filter through for the next in line.

Lewis paced about impatiently, checking the straps on the packs, breaking open the shotgun and snapping it closed, studying the heat-pulsing rocks and sun-hammered country.

'Godforsaken hellhole,' he opined. 'C'mon. Let's get outa here.'

Grant heaved to his feet. 'I'll start loading the mules that've already had a drink. You two could saddle-up and be ready if you're in such a hurry.'

They camped in the shadow of Sabre Peak the following day and Grant, after setting up things for the hunters, told them he would ride back to the dry wash where he was to meet Dog and the other man Barnett was expecting.

'Before you go,' Barnett said, taking his hand-drawn map from his jacket pocket and unfolding it. 'Take a look at this.'

Grant walked across, aware that Lewis was watching narrowly as he took the square of well-creased paper from Barnett. There was a crude drawing of what appeared to be a mesa as seen from above, but one side seemed to have collapsed and there was a

U-shaped shaded portion at the base of what Grant figured was meant to be a huge rockpile. He looked at Barnett.

'No names on the landmarks – and whoever drew this was no artist.'

Barnett smiled crookedly. 'Personally, I think he did quite well, considering the circumstances...'

Grant heard Lewis chuckle. 'Circumstances?' he asked.

'Mmm. Man was dying, had a couple of bullets in him and he'd been tortured by the Apaches. But he was a grateful soul, held on long enough to draw this and give it to the people who tried to rescue him.'

'Too late to do him much good by the sounds of it,' Grant opined dryly.

'You're right there,' Barnett agreed. 'Could that mesa be your Hell's Doorway?'

Grant started. 'Beats me. I've never seen the place, nor heard of the actual location for that matter. Just that it's somewhere in this neck of the woods.' He looked closely at Barnett, saw the anxiety and expectancy on the man's face, edged with disappointment. 'You think the story's true about the wagon train being swallowed-up?'

Barnett took back the map, not yet folding it up. He made a half-sceptical, half-uncertain grimace. 'I'd really like to find out, Bronco.'

Grant scrubbed a hand around his bristled jaw. 'That why you've got all those ropes and shackles? You aim to find the sinkhole and – go down into it?'

'Well, perhaps not me personally. D'you think you can locate the mesa from this map?'

Grant was silent a long time. He was uneasy about them confiding in him. There was no real reason for it at this stage ... or was there? He'd already seen the climbing gear so he would've been able to piece things together at some time. Maybe they figured they might as well come clean now.

There would have to be a lot more, of course, but in any case, he couldn't see these two cutting him in for a share of whatever it was they were after. And that meant they wouldn't let him ride away with the information he had just been given...

He was suddenly aware that they were waiting for his answer. 'Well, I don't know that I could locate it, but I'll ask Dog what he knows about it when I see him.'

Barnett frowned. 'He won't come to our camp here? Not even if I offer him more money?'

'Money means nothing to Dog.'

'Oh, is that so? He dickered forty bucks out of me to go fetch our third man!'

Grant smiled thinly. 'He'll likely give it to me. He just saw it as a chance to get a few more dollars for me. He has no use for money. And that draw where I'm s'posed to meet him is as far as Dog'll come. Even that's really too far for him, too close to what he calls the devil land.'

'What you might call trail's end for him?' queried Lewis, and he made a choking sound which suddenly turned into a cough.

Grant looked at him sharply. He was sure

the man was smiling as if at some secret joke behind that hand covering his mouth...

Dog was waiting with the third man in the shade of the northern wall of the draw.

The man's name was Ray Sinclair and Grant was surprised to see he was only in his twenties, pale, but he seemed very fit. There was one packhorse with bulging, tarp-covered packs, and Sinclair's outdoor clothes – checked flannel shirt, wide-brimmed hat, dark-brown corduroy trousers tucked into scratched but polished halfboots – looked brand new under their film of trail dust. So did the Colt Peace-maker in the leather holster on the belt that still smelled of neatsfoot oil and dressing. The cartridges in the loops glinted brightly in the sun. Fresh from the ammunition carton.

Sinclair's face was narrow and he was good looking, though his jaw seemed on the weak side. He was ready enough to smile but it had a tight edge to it and his hand grip was quick, just a squeeze.

'Rafe and Harve not coming?' Sinclair asked Grant, looking behind the man as if he expected to see the others riding in.

'We're camped at the foot of Sabre Peak,' Grant told him. 'Why don't you saddle up, Mr Sinclair, while I have a word with Dog?'

'Sure thing – and call me Ray.'

'Fine with me, Ray.' Grant jerked his head at the Apache and they walked down the slope into the bottom of the draw.

'Know anything about him, Dog?'

The Apache shrugged. 'Asked Potter in livery while I chose a packhorse. He say Sinclair came in on train, booked into Colorado, spent all night gambling at Elkhorn.'

Sy Witherspoon's Elkhorn Saloon was known far and wide along the cattle trails for its gambling, Witherspoon having imported many of his tables and operators from back East. He ran the highest-stakes games west of Denver and some said he was only a front for an Eastern gambling syndicate. True or not, Witherspoon was likely the richest man in the territory at that time.

'Anything else?' Grant asked.

'He's no greenhorn. Can ride, make camp, track jack-rabbit for supper ... but lousy shot.'

'He looks fit enough, but there's not enough tan to make me think he works out of doors.'

The Apache hesitated. 'He tell me what he is – big name. Can't say it. He go into caves.' Grant arched his eyebrows and Dog said quickly, 'Bronco, this bad country here. You come out. Soon.'

'Soon as I can, Dog, but I've got to earn that two hundred first.' He quickly explained about the mesa and Hell's Doorway and Dog hissed as he sucked in air through his broken teeth.

He placed a hand on Grant's forearm. 'Come now. That place *very* bad. *Muy malo, amigo!* Forget money, you come.' He tugged on Grant's arm but the horse rancher shook his head, a mite surprised at seeing Dog so anxious and concerned.

'Gave my word, Dog.'

The Apache released his grip, stared levelly into Grant's face. 'This one time you should break it.'

'Can't, Dog.'

Dog sighed. 'I know. You wouldn't be Bronco Grant if you did. But be careful, *mi amigo*. I wait for you at dry waterfall. Three day.'

'I'll try to be there by then, Dog, if not, you go tell Fergus Perry what's been happening. And the ranch is yours.'

Dog's dark eyes searched Grant's face. 'You my blood-brother, Bronco. I am ashamed I – I can not stay with you.'

Grant clapped a hand to the Indian's shoulder, forced a grin. 'No shame in it, Dog. I don't like the feel of this country myself. I'll be out in three days if I can manage it. You take care.'

Dog grunted, mounted up and rode out of the dry wash, lifting a hand in farewell without looking back. Lewis turned as Sinclair led up his saddled mount, looking after the Apache.

'Aw, wanted to say so-long to him. Fascinatin' people, the Apaches. Running Dog seems like a fine example of 'em.'

Grant smiled easily at this likeable young man who seemed to have a weakness for gambling. 'Yeah, Dog's a good man. Well, we'd best be riding.'

They mounted and Grant took the lead rope of the packhorse, noticing how the animal moved.

'Those packs are pretty big but don't seem to have all that much weight in them, Ray.'

Sinclair smiled, looking more boyish than ever. 'Mostly tarps, that's why.' At Grant's puzzled look, his smile widened. 'An old miner's trick – when you've got to work in long dark tunnels or down deep shafts, often an oil lamp, or even half a dozen, isn't enough. These tarps are all pure white. We string 'em so they catch the sun and reflect the light in to where you're working. Or as far as you can make it go. Of course, you eventually get into darkness beyond the reach of reflected light but the tarps help a helluva lot, believe me. They're bulky but not too heavy to pack.'

'Smart idea,' Grant said slowly, knowing that Sinclair had just given him a hint of what kind of work he was coming to do for Lewis and Barnett. The man must be some kind of mining specialist, he guessed, but Sinclair did seem a mite on the edgy side for that kind of profession, even though he was working hard at appearing relaxed. After they cleared the wash, Grant asked casually, 'Known Lewis and Barnett long?'

'Just the few weeks I was in Denver.' He grinned. 'Couldn't resist when they asked me if I'd like to join them on this expedition.'

'Know what it's all about?'

Sinclair continued to look uncomfortable. 'Reckon you'd best ask Rafe for details, Bronco, I don't know everything myself. I'm really only interested in descending into a sinkhole: never been down one before.'

Grant let it go. Sinclair obviously wanted to change the subject and he listened politely as the young caver went into a series of stories about his adventures under-ground.

When they reached the camp at the base of Sabre Peak, Barnett greeted them and young Sinclair seemed awkward and a mite nervous as he shook hands.

Grant looked about him. 'Where's Lewis?'

Barnett looked up from speaking to the caver. 'Oh, Harve went to see if he could scare up a jack-rabbit. Fancies a stew, he said.'

Barnett turned back to his conversation with Ray Sinclair and Grant felt a sudden lurch in his belly as he looked towards Lewis's pile of gear amongst the rocks he had chosen as his part of the camp.

The shotgun was missing. And any rabbit hit with a blast from that wouldn't leave enough to feed a cat let alone make supper for four men.

It was drawing into late afternoon and Running Dog was not yet clear of the land he thought of as being bad-medicine country, although the *real* devil land was actually a few miles behind him – but this was close enough to bother him.

He was a brave warrior in every respect, and he had taken some of the white man's ways during the years he had served as an army scout and the time he had spent with Bronco Grant.

But he still held to his Apache upbringing, still avoided owls as bearers of ill-omen – his skin actually prickled if he heard one hoot during a night camp in strange country. And when he returned to sacred home country he always felt impelled – as did the Old Ones – to climb down from his horse and pay his respects to the Four Worlds – Fire to the east, Air to the south, Water to the west, Light to the north.

This latter was the most important because it was the Light of the Great Spirit, the Giver-Of-All, *Ysin*.

In the night, he sometimes spoke to the spirits, believing that every man rode to his gods by way of a trail of his own choosing – and they were all images of One. So, while Dog lived mostly in the white-man's world these days, he had never really left that of the red man.

His beliefs conjured up terrifying visions, painted for him in colourful words by the elders of the tribe when he was only a child, but planted indelibly in his brain so that they would be with him until the moment of his death.

He glanced up at the sun, saw it was heeled far over, knew it would pass behind the peaks before he had cleared this hellish country and the thought of being still within its bounds when darkness fell set his heart hammering.

It was because of the old beliefs surging through his brain that Running Dog was not aware that he was being followed.

More than that: the man who had been

behind him for so many miles had now passed him, on the far side of a ridge, and was waiting for the lone Apache to appear in the shadowed pass that eventually led out of the devil country.

Dog, nostrils flared, every sense alert for the first signs of the evil spirits he felt were all around him, knew nothing of the man who had come to kill him until the cold, mocking voice spoke from the edge of the trail to his right and slightly above him.

'You ain't gonna make it – Yallerdog!'

Dog reined down his pinto sharply, gasping as the words shook him out of his state of fear. *A white-man's voice!* No spirit, good or bad, would use such a subterfuge, so it must indeed be a white man ... and a hated one at that!

He recognized Harve Lewis immediately, saw the man standing atop a sharp-angled rock, holding the big twin-barrelled shotgun, pointing in his general direction.

Lewis grinned tightly. 'Too bad, ain't it, Yallerdog? You're gonna die on the devil land. No hope of goin' to the happy hunting ground then, is there? Your spirit's gonna wander forever between the winds, unable to reach your heathen god! And, I'll tell you somethin' else, after I kill you, I'm gonna shoot your eyes out, so you'll be blind and won't *never* be able to find your way into the next world! How you like that, you stinkin' Apache?'

Dog said nothing and his flat, emotionless face showed nothing. But his heart was hammering and his brain felt as if it was going to boil. Such threats as Lewis made were terrifying to him: he believed an Apache could only hope for a good reception in the next world if he died in battle, with the blood of a bitter enemy fresh on his hands. But to be killed on evil land like this and then have his eyes shot out...!

He wanted to scream to *Ysin* for help – but knew that an Apache in this world had to help himself.

And there was only one way left to him now: he knew he could not escape the blast of Lewis's shotgun, but he could make his try at dying like a true Apache – with the blood of an enemy dripping from his hands in his last convulsion.

The sudden cry hammering and echoing from the walls of the narrow pass startled Lewis and chilled his blood so that his skin prickled in a surging wave from scalp to toenails. It froze him, his thumb on the hammer, finger on the trigger, immovable for a moment.

It was all that Dog needed. He leapt the pinto forward and up the slope, whipping out his hunting knife, still screaming his death cry as he slashed at Lewis's lower legs which were at about his eyelevel as he charged past the rock where the white man stood.

Lewis screamed in pain as the blade cut through the leather of his halfboots, sliced into his flesh. He fell as Dog thundered on down the pass. On the ground, Lewis rolled, panting, the shock passing now, replaced by rage.

He thumbed back a gun hammer, fired, saw Dog lurch, swore because it was the buckshot barrel and not the one with the slug he had fired. He wanted that goddamn Apache *blown apart!*

Breathing hard, hands shaking, he fumbled at the second hammer, fired as Dog lurched around a bend. The heavy slug exploded a rock next to the man and then he was gone, the pinto's hoofs fading down the pass.

Painfully, Lewis staggered forward, reloading, but when he rounded the shattered rock there was no sign of either the Apache or his pinto. Only many splashes of bright blood on the rocks and the ground.

'Die, you Injun bastard!' he gasped. 'Die slow...!'

## 6

## Mystery Mesa

Supper consisted of venison that Dog had jerked Indian-fashion and coffee. It was dark when the meal was over and Grant was smoking a cheroot and sipping coffee when he heard the sound of a horse approaching.

He snatched up his rifle and had already stepped back out of the firelight before the other two had moved. Lewis appeared, slumped in the saddle, one bloody, gashed boot dangling from the horn, his lower left leg crudely bandaged.

Barnett and Sinclair ran to him, got him down and stretched out by the fire. Ray fussed with the bandages and prepared hot water as Grant strolled across and asked harshly, 'What happened, Lewis?'

The injured man looked up with pain-filled eyes. 'Ran into a coupla bucks way back in the hills. Nailed 'em both but one got me with a knife.'

'That dry wash where I met Dog and Ray is as close as any Indian'll come to this country.'

'The hell with you, Grant! I told you what happened!'

Grant said nothing, fetched needle and twine from his saddle-bags and stitched the large, deep wound. 'Best keep it clean or you could lose that leg,' he told Lewis flatly.

Next morning, Lewis's leg was inflamed and swollen and he refused breakfast but drank some coffee, said he was able to sit a horse.

Grant took bearings from a knoll and they set off towards the south-west. He had an uneasy feeling that all was not well with Dog, kept glaring at Lewis. The wounded man slowed them down but the following day they sighted the mesa in the distance around mid-morning.

Sabre Peak was visible through the haze off to one side, a triangular rock formation that glinted in the sun.

Barnett was excited and even Lewis, despite his pain, brightened at sight of the mesa. Barnett brought out his map and Sinclair, flushed and animated, rode his horse in close. Grant leaned sideways to see as Barnett pointed to the map.

'See this U-shaped place shaded in? Apparently some years back one side of the mesa caved-in because there was a sinkhole very close to the edge. It opened it up down one side and formed a cavern that makes the shaft accessible from ground level, from inside the cave itself.' He tapped the creased paper. 'That's our way in – and down.'

Grant looked at the others soberly. 'I'd say it's time for some explanations, gents. You obviously sent Chick in to pick a fight with me to see how tough I was. You've hassled and prodded me all the way in here, bribed me to bring you to this mesa – and separated me from Dog. Now what?'

He stiffened at the sound of a gun hammer cocking, spun in the saddle, hand slapping his gun butt, but froze when he saw the smirking Lewis holding the shotgun on him.

'Got a slug in each barrel, Grant. Which would you like? Left or right?' He was a lot more alert than he had made out.

'Harve!' snapped Barnett.

'Hell, why pussyfoot around any longer, Rafe? We're here now. We don't need Grant any longer. I seen you taking note of landmarks coming in, you can lead us out, can't you?'

Barnett nodded. 'Yeah,' he agreed slowly. 'But we still need Grant. There's a lot of work to be done.'

'So, take his guns and we make him do what Ray wants. Hell, he's nothing in this deal now we're here!'

Sinclair licked his lips. 'Now, just a minute, gents, I wasn't told there'd be anything like this!'

'You weren't told a lot of things, kid!'

snapped Lewis. 'But you do what Rafe and me want and you got no worries. But, play it safe: hand over your sixgun to Rafe.'

Ray looked at Grant who nodded slowly and after Barnett had Sinclair's weapon the man took Grant's Colt and seemed to relax some.

'Why all the tests? Chick, Lewis riding me and so on?'

'Just getting an idea of what we were gonna be up against when we told you where we really wanted to go,' Barnett told him. 'It was the boss's idea. He likes to know *exactly* how tough and smart his enemy is.'

'This boss got a name?'

'Not one that'd mean anything to you. Let's get around to the far side of the mesa and take a look at the cavern,' Barnett said, gesturing curtly with Grant's cocked Colt.

They rode around and found that almost half of one face of the mesa had slid down and piled-up in a steep ramp of earth studded with shattered rocks. Beyond it was the dark oval of the cave's entrance and Sinclair dismounted without waiting for orders and clambered up. Panting, he looked over the top, smiling as he turned to call down to the others.

'The collapse has reduced the depth by at least fifty feet but it's still the devil of a long way down!'

'He could be down there, waiting, kid!' Lewis cracked. 'After all, it's s'posed to be a way into Hell!'

'We'll need to clear a way to the cave,' Sinclair said, sliding down in a cloud of dust. 'Then we'll need some long poles. Those lodgepoles growing on that ridge yonder ought to be all right.'

'OK,' Barnett snapped, sounding impatient now. 'Bronco, you give Ray a hand, whatever he wants. You want to argue – well, I wouldn't, was I you. Understand?'

The second long pine box contained digging tools, shovels with long and short handles, forks, picks, crowbars. Grant and Sinclair used most of these as they sweated and strained hour after hour to dig a narrow trail in through the huge pile of dirt and rocks.

When they were through, black from head to foot with dirt and sweat, Sinclair picked up two rocks, staggered into the cave and dropped them over the edge of the sinkhole that plunged away deep into the earth, full of impenetrable blackness.

'By God, I thought I heard a splash!' Ray called. 'Must be water down there. Could mean an underground river, or what's left of one.' Soberly he added, 'Might've washed some of the debris away, though the gold'd be too heavy...'

'Shut up, kid!' growled Barnett. 'It's getting dark. You two wash up and you can go cut the lodgepoles first thing tomorrow. You're going to work your butts off from now on.'

Down at the small creek that ran out of one wall of the mesa, Ray said the water was so clear and pure because it was rain that had fallen as long as fifty years ago but had only now filtered down through the lime-stone of the mesa.

'That why there's an underground river?' Grant asked.

'Maybe, but more likely to be one that has its source hundreds of miles away.' The kid sounded tense and Grant knew it was because of the next logical question.

'What gold, kid? I've never heard of any gold being found in this part of Colorado.'

'No. Not like at Cherry Creek or Creede, not alluvial or gold-bearing ore, but there's gold down there just the same.' He sobered and his teeth tugged at his lower lip as he added softly, 'At least, by God, I hope so!'

Grant abruptly snapped his fingers. 'Hell, that old story about the sinkhole swallowing a whole wagon train! Is that it?'

Ray held his gaze, nodded gently, then took a surreptitious glance under his arm at Barnett and Lewis who were watching closely. 'I better not say any more.'

'You damn well better had, Ray! Or neither of us are gonna get outa this!'

Sinclair swallowed, hesitated, lowered his voice. 'All right, just the outline. My uncle was part of an escort of Confederate soldiers bringing two wagonloads of gold back to the South for the last-ditch stand. In 1864 Indians attacked and on the mesa the sinkhole opened up, taking wagons and men – including Indians – down into the earth. My uncle was one of two survivors. The other man died soon after Uncle Ned got him out. Ned eventually made it out of this country but was captured by Indians. Yankees sweeping south rescued him but because of the torture he'd been through, he lost a leg and the stump developed gangrene.'

Barnett and Lewis were stirring impatiently now and Sinclair began to speak faster. 'He knew he was dying, and he drew that map Barnett has, put it in an envelope and addressed it to my father. The Yankees must've thought it was his Will or something because they mailed it, but what with the chaos after the war it was almost two years before it arrived. By that time my father was dead, too. I didn't know what it was all about although I'd heard rumours about the Rebel gold that'd been lost.' He paused and sighed. 'I just put it in a drawer.

'To cut it short, Bronco, I took to gambling when I grew up and not long ago a woman named Donna set me up for a fleecing in Denver. I'd made out I was well-heeled, you see, so's to get credit.' He shook his head sadly. 'The stupidity of it! Well, you can guess: I lost, I couldn't pay and they beat me up, ransacked my room looking for valuables and found the map. I saw it as my way out, told the story in elaborate but exaggerated detail and said there was *definitely* gold in the sinkhole. Barnett's boss, himself a gambler, said he was willing to take a chance and accepted the map in payment of my debts. He was a Reb officer. I think he knew about the wagons.'

Grant frowned. 'Then what the hell're you doing here?'

Ray Sinclair looked mighty sheepish. 'I'm

a part-time speleologist – most folk can't pronounce it so the general word is "spellunker"...?' His voice rose expectantly.

Grant frowned. 'Don't look at me. I've never heard of it.'

Ray smiled nervously. 'I go down into caves and map them, check them out for safety and so on. I need money to gamble with, you see. Anyway, I was stupid enough to ask if I could come along. I've never been down a genuine sinkhole and I offered my services to recover the gold in exchange for the chance to go down.'

'You must be plumb loco, Ray!'

He nodded. 'I can see that now. But I was so relieved to be given a clean slate I just ... got carried away. I wish now, of course, I'd kept my mouth shut.' Then they threw themselves apart as Lewis's shotgun roared like a clap of thunder and large chunks of rock and clods of earth raked them stingingly.

'Get the hell up here right *now!* Both of you! There's too much damn palavering going on! Now *move!*'

Next morning, they were given axes and were taken up to the ridge where the tall lodgepole pine trees grew.

'I reckon we'll need about six,' Sinclair said, rubbing his wrists which still bore the marks of the ropes that had tied him up last night. 'Twelve feet minimum, straight as you can get, six inches across at the base tapering to no less than four. They might have to bear a deal of weight.'

Barnett sat with the mules and horses in the shade of some trees overhanging a circle of rocks. Lewis, limping badly, his face screwed with pain, dragged himself closer to where Ray and Grant were working. He perched on a rock, letting his wounded leg dangle, shotgun across his lap, jacket pockets sagging with extra shells.

'No palavering!' he snapped. 'Just get them trees cut and trimmed and back to the cave pronto!' Then, while he was looking steadily at Grant with his hot, hating eyes, he added, 'Just try something, Grant. I'd love to blow off one of your goddamn legs!'

He slapped the flat of a hand against his shotgun. Grant said nothing, turned to the stand of trees, chose one and shrugged out of his shirt, spat into his palms, and commenced chopping. Sinclair chose a stand several yards to his right, hefted the axe and began swinging it rhythmically.

Chips flew as the sharp blades bit into the soft wood and the first two trees came crashing down within seconds of each other. One branch almost swept Lewis's rock and he cursed Ray Sinclair.

'That happens again and I'll shoot you in the foot! You'll still be able to go down the rope and hook on the gold.'

'I didn't see that branch hanging out to the side,' Ray said defensively. 'I'm sorry, Mr Lewis.'

'You just watch it, kid,' the man growled, and threw Grant a glare. 'The hell're you looking at? Get that next tree cut down!'

Grant hefted his axe and moved around the tree a little for a better swing, undercut his original slice, then moved back and drove the blade deep into the wood, several times. The slim tree shook and fibres creaked and cracked as it began a slow lean. Sinclair was slicing into his own tree, glanced up to see how Grant was doing, willing to make a contest out of this. He froze and his mouth opened to call a warning, but no words came and his eyes widened as he watched Grant's tree sag outwards into another close by, the tops briefly entangling before the cut tree twisted off at the base with a sound like a series of pistol shots – and then fell straight for Lewis's seat.

The man was watching Sinclair because his axe had stopped swinging and he began to curse and threaten the caver when the shadow of Grant's falling tree flitted across him. He snapped his head up, face pale, and he yelled in terror as he flung himself wildly off the rock, arms covering his head as he dropped the shotgun and spilled to ground, jarring his leg.

The splintering crash drowned his cries as the tree smashed across the rock where he had been sitting, burying him under a mass of thrashing branches.

Barnett had been alerted by all the noise, jumped up, sixgun in hand, yelling as he saw Grant already disappearing into the stand of timber. He fired and bullets ripped bark and sprayed sap as Grant zigzagged, going upslope. Barnett ran for the horses, leapt into his own saddle with surprising agility for an overweight man, and spurred up the slope.

Dazed, but flooding anger taking charge now, Lewis roared erect through the broken branches, tugging wildly at his shotgun. He blasted a shot up the slope and a branch shattered and hung by a strip of bark. He fired again and the slug made a roaring sound as it tore through foliage above the running Grant's head.

Sinclair had frozen, was still holding the handle of his axe with the blade buried in the trunk of the tree. Lewis, muttering as he broke open the gun and fumbled out fresh loads, leapt at him despite his wounded leg, cried out in pain as he landed and then swung the gun butt in a vicious arc. Sinclair fell like a poled steer, blood dribbling from the fresh cut across his forehead. He lay there moaning as Lewis limped across the slope, shouting at Barnett to ride to the left and cut off Grant.

Grant was smashing at the foliage with his arms, keeping it away from his face. A bullet ricocheted from a tree trunk only a yard to his left and he saw Barnett's horse just below him on the slope, pacing him, the man using his knees and allowing the horse its head more or less as it weaved between the lodgepoles. He fired as Grant's body flashed across a small clearing and Grant stopped, startled, as the lead cut air in front of his face.

The abrupt change of pace made him lose balance and he fell, tried to get his feet under him, but his boots skidded on the steep slope. He crashed backwards, arms flailing as he tried to grab saplings or bushes as they slid past while he skidded down the grade.

Barnett spurred towards him, smoking gun coming down to bead him, the man's face white with anger. Then Grant felt a dead branch under his grasping hands, closed his fingers around it, dug in his heels and allowed his momentum to jerk him half upright.

Barnett wasn't expecting it, was still aiming low and his bullet punched into the ground between Grant's boots. Then Grant hurled the dead branch and Barnett threw up his arms as it smashed into him, glanced off his head and sent him spilling out of the saddle.

Grant fell to hands and knees, pushed up and lunged for the flying reins of the rearing horse. Lewis's shotgun thundered and the heavy bear-killer slug smashed a path through low slung branches, severing them, but ploughing on, undeflected because of its low speed and massive weight.

Grant threw himself flat between the horse's legs and rolled several feet. He bounced up and ran left, heard the shotgun roar again and a fist-sized chunk was blown out of the tree a foot to his right. He shielded his face with a raised arm, was about to leap away, but suddenly changed his mind, leapt over Barnett's struggling figure, lurching as the man clawed at his legs. Grant kicked him in the head, pounded across and up the slope, intent on reaching Lewis before the man could reload the shotgun. The weapon was broken at the breech, he had removed the used shells, was fumbling two out of his jacket pocket, looking wild-eyed towards Grant's charging figure as he rammed them home, snapped the gun closed and started to lift it.

Grant was upon him, knocking the barrels aside, one firing wildly, bringing a whinny of terror from the horse. He wrenched the weapon from Lewis's hands, swung the barrels back-handed and caught the man across the side of the head.

Lewis, already unsteady on his feet, went down and Grant knelt with a knee on the man's chest, cocked the gun and rammed the barrels under the dazed killer's jaw.

'What've you done to Running Dog, you son of a bitch?' he snarled, ramming hard with the barrels, making Lewis choke. 'Tell me or by God I'll blow your head clear off your body right now!'

'I don't think so, Bronco!'

Sweat stung Grant's eyes as he started to swing his head towards the sound of Barnett's voice and then there was a faint whistling sound and something smashed across his head with what felt like enough force to crack his skull open like an over-ripe melon. He didn't remember tumbling forward to plough his face into the slope.

When he came round, swimming up slowly as if through a lake of honey, his head pounding and throbbing, he found he was propped up against the tree he had deliberately felled so that it crashed on to

Lewis's rock.

His vision was going in and out of focus and he couldn't make out the words of the angry voices that yelled at him. But he felt the jolting blows of hard boot toes and rifle butts slamming into his aching body.

Then he heard Barnett's commanding voice. 'Enough, Harve, goddamnit, *enough!* He's no good to us as a cripple.'

Grant could just make out the wild-eyed sagging Lewis, panting as he leaned on his crutch, holding his shotgun by the barrels, half-raised as if to club him again. Then the man leaned down close to Grant's battered face and he smiled tightly.

'You were asking about Dog? Well, I blew off his left arm at the shoulder, peppered his back with buckshot. He managed to stay in the saddle and rode off – but you can just think about how long it's gonna take the red bastard to die! Huh? How you like that?'

He swung the gun and clipped Grant's jaw, sending the man back into oblivion.

# 7

## Mesa Mayhem

When he came round again, he could tell it was afternoon and he felt as if he had just been through a cattle stampede. He propped himself up on one elbow, saw he was back at the camp, just outside the cavern. Barnett was sitting on a big rock inside the entrance while Lewis was stretched out on his blankets, his bandaged leg propped up on a saddle. He hefted his shotgun, letting Grant know he was being watched.

From inside the cavern came the sounds of digging.

Barnett saw he was awake. 'Go down to the creek and soak your head, then get up here and help Sinclair rig those poles. You try anything else and we'll kill you instantly. If you do manage to get away, we'll kill Ray...'

'Like hell you will,' Grant slurred, standing groggily. 'You need him more than me.'

'Thing is, Bronco, we can find our way out of here any time. If we have to kill you both, we'll just go back and get some more men and come out here again and bring up whatever's down that shaft. Fact is, we don't really need either of you now; we're holding the winning hand.'

Grant had to agree that they did and he stumbled his way down to the creek and plunged into the chill waters, gasping, but glad of the numbing cold on his wounds and aches.

Inside the cavern, he helped Sinclair dig holes for the bases of the six poles the man had cut while Grant had been unconscious. They let them come together over the dark maw of the sinkhole, the tops interlocking like a *tipi* frame. Ray got ropes up there, lashed them tightly, fastened on his blocks and pulleys and a ratchet arrangement that he said would take three-quarters of the weight of any object slung from the rope, making it easier to haul up. He hooked on a leather bosun's chair and then they rigged the white canvas strips on adjustable ropes so they could catch the strongest sunlight and reflect it down the shaft.

Grant felt dizzy as he looked over the crumbling edge, saw the broken walls, smelled the dankness like the breath of Satan himself. Ray took them all through the series of signals he would use on the rope once he was in the shaft: one tug meant he was on the bottom and unstrapped from the bosun's chair; two tugs meant he was ready to come up; three – that was the emergency signal and they were to haul him up as quickly as they could.

'I don't know what I'm going to find down there,' Ray finished, sounding surprisingly calm. 'There may be an unsound bottom, the walls might cave in, there could be snakes or animals. Just get me up fast if you feel three tugs, Bronco.'

'You've got my word on it, Ray,' Grant assured him and Sinclair spoke to Barnett.

'You might have to give Bronco a hand, Mr Barnett.'

'Sure, sure, we'll all pitch in,' Barnett said, jumpy with impatience. 'Now you get on down there and see what you can find!'

'And no pussyfooting around!' growled Lewis, his eyes bright with fever, face flushed, looking like a death's head. 'That gold's been down there long enough. Bring it up into the light of day quick as you can.'

'I'll just have to see what it's like when I get down there,' Sinclair said quietly, but firmly. 'I'm going to have to play it by ear, Mr Lewis. I have no choice.'

Lewis's shotgun inched around. 'Just ... get ... it ... done!' Ray jumped at the snarled words and the way the shotgun's barrels jerked. 'No more delays, goddamnit! Get your harness and ropes ready, you're going down there right now, kid!'

'It's getting on for sundown,' Grant pointed out and it earned him a sharp poke in the spine with Barnett's sixgun.

'So what, Bronco? No matter what time he goes down, it's going to be blacker than the inside of a hibernating bear down there.'

Sinclair sighed. 'I'm afraid he's right, Bronco. Well, I might as well go see what's down there, I guess.' Actually, Sinclair was keen enough to go down because this would be a first for him, a descent into a genuine sinkhole. But Grant knew the man hadn't really thought it through: like what would happen if there was no gold down there?

Or – even if there was!

Grant could see that Lewis and Barnett wouldn't have a lot of use for himself *or* Sinclair once the gold bars were up on the surface...

He had no chance to mention this to Sinclair, but there would be no point in doing so anyway. The one thing he did ask as he helped Ray on with his harness was the name of Barnett's boss.

Ray looked startled, saw the others watching and as he leaned forward to buckle up a strap, said one word softly: Grant wasn't sure if it was 'Hallows' or 'Fallows' or even 'Fellows'.

Then Sinclair, lowering his burning reflector lantern and tying its yard-length rope to one side of the chair so that it dangled, took the two spare, unlit lanterns Grant handed him and kicked away from the edge. Crumbling soil and small stones pattered and clattered down the hundred-foot deep shaft. The depth was only Ray's estimation; he said it could be a lot deeper. Grant lowered away, adjusting his speed to commands called up by Sinclair. Lewis and Barnett grew excited when he called a halt and examined something caught on the shaft's side.

'Could be several old rotted hides.' His voice boomed and echoed through the cavern.

'By God! The buffalo hides from the wagons!' gasped Barnett. 'I don't think I really believed it before, Harve, but – man! It sounds as if the story's true! The wagons did go in here!'

'But were they carrying gold bullion or was that just something Ray's uncle added to make it a good story?'

Grant earned himself some cold glares, but he knew they wouldn't attack him while he was still lowering Sinclair. It took another ten minutes before Ray reached the bottom, the burning lantern a mere speck of light. One tug jerked the rope and they knew he was on the bottom and out of the chair. He lit the other two lanterns and, one in each hand, called out he was entering a side tunnel that was half-blocked with debris.

'Must've been some flash floods through here over the years.' That's what they thought he said, anyway: the shaft and the cavern roof distorted his words.

The three men up top waited, scarcely breathing, peering cautiously over the edge. There was a rising scream that chilled their blood, followed by a whirring sound and they reared back, startled, as hundreds of bats exploded out of the shaft and filled the cavern with screeching before pouring out like a black waterspout from the entrance into the darkening sky.

Hearts pounding they strained to hear as Sinclair called up again. Even with the distortion they could detect the edge of excitement in his voice.

'Wreckage ... skeletons ... old rusted percussion weapons. All jammed in a recess – by flood waters is my guess.

'The gold, damnit!' bawled Lewis, sweating and coughing occasionally, absently rubbing his swollen leg. Grant knew a fever was taking over which meant infection.

There was silence after Lewis's words boomed away. It dragged on. They heard a couple of clunks echoing down there. Then Ray's voice, breathless now.

'It's here!' His voice cracked as he yelled. 'You've never seen anything like it! A ... it's like ... like scattered fire! Gold bars as bright as the day they were minted. A pile here, a bigger one there ... a line of others. The wagon beds have been smashed by the fall and it looks as if there were false bottoms and the gold has spilled out. There must ... millions.'

Lewis and Barnett were strangely silent, stunned most likely, like Grant, for he had, until this moment doubted the story, figured it to be just another of those legends that build up from an actual happening as a starting point but become embellished as it is told year after year...

'Send it up!' Lewis croaked, strangling on the thought of all that gold. 'Send up the goddamn gold, kid!'

'That'll take days, maybe a week!' Ray called. 'The bars are heavy and even with the ratchet the rope'll only take so much weight – only a couple of bars at a time, I'd say and there must be at least a hundred here, likely much more.'

Barnett blew out his cheeks, wiped a hand across his suddenly sweating forehead. His eyes were bright, Grant noticed and his fingers were bloodless where they gripped the edge of the shaft.

'Send up a couple of samples, Ray,' he called in a surprisingly controlled voice now, friendly, coercing.

'I'll put two bars in the chair. You'll have to haul up carefully, Bronco, or they'll spill out.'

Barnett smiled and actually winked at Grant. Lewis was still scowling down into the shaft. 'Hurry it up !'

Then Ray called, 'I'm coming up with them ... that'll be best. I can hold the bars in my lap then, but it'll take a couple of men on the ropes.'

Barnett's smile vanished suddenly and Lewis swore, lifted the shotgun threateningly, pointing it down the shaft.

'Don't fire that!' snapped Grant. 'The concussion could collapse the entire shaft, seal it off forever. There'd be no chance of you getting the gold then.'

Lewis swung the gun towards Grant. 'You

want to go down there without the rope?'

'Only if you come with me.'

'Shut up, both of you!' snapped Barnett. 'Ray! You just send up the samples and stay put. We can get up a lot more before we quit tonight.'

A long silence. Lewis cursed as it dragged on.

'What the hell's he doing?' he growled.

'Maybe he found another way out,' Grant suggested but it only earned him a backhand blow across the face from the angry Barnett.

'Ray! Send up that gold! Or we'll throw Grant down! We don't really need him, I can work the rope. You hear me, boy?'

'All right,' Ray Sinclair called up, voice a mite shaky. 'I-I'll load the bars onto the chair.'

Grant said nothing, even kept his throbbing face blank, but the hatred for these men was raging inside him.

Ray sent up two bars and, as he had said, they were mint-bright, *alive*, gleaming with that special aura that has fascinated men since the first nugget was found in some still, primeval pool.

Lewis and Barnett handled the bars almost reverently, constantly running their trembling hands over the gold. Grant was alert for a chance to grab a weapon but Barnett kept enough control to make sure it never happened.

'Send up some more!' Lewis bawled. 'Fast!'

Ray obeyed. Grant hauled up four more bars and then it was very dark inside the cavern, no more sunlight outside to reflect from the canvas strips. Lamps were inadequate and Barnett reluctantly decided to call it a day.

'Send down the bosun's chair, then,' Ray called.

Grant made the feather chair ready, but Barnett reached out, pushed him aside and shook his head. Lewis covered him with his shotgun, smirking.

Barnett called down the shaft. 'Be best if

you stay down there for the night, Ray. Save all this hauling and busting our backs. You'll be all right. We can drop you down a little jerky if you're hungry and you already have water...'

'No!' Ray's panicky voice boomed up the shaft. 'No, don't leave me down here all night! There're snakes.'

'Cuddle up to one – it'll keep you warm!' Lewis laughed wildly and it sounded mad as it echoed down the shaft.

'You bastards!' Grant said, and Lewis rounded on him.

'You climb down that rope and keep him company, Grant! Go on! Do it or I'll blow you apart!'

'Easy, Harve,' Barnett said. 'I don't want those two together. There just might be another way out. We'll tie Grant up tonight.'

'Bring Ray up and tie him to a tree, too,' Grant said. 'He's done everything you wanted. Don't leave him down there with snakes, for Chrissakes!'

Sinclair was shouting up the shaft, almost

pleading now, asking over and over to be brought up. Barnett leaned over carefully.

'See you in the morning, kid!'

Grant suddenly spun towards the small stack of gold bars near the edge of the shaft. He skidded under Lewis's gun and kicked at the pile. All six bars tumbled back down the shaft.

'Watch out, Ray!' Grant yelled, rolling away quickly as Lewis fired and the slug chewed a hefty chunk out of the edge.

Barnett screamed at Lewis to hold his fire, brought up his sixgun and triggered at Grant. The man shoulder-rolled, kicked at Lewis's wounded leg and the killer screamed as he collapsed. Grant bounced to his feet and ran out into the darkness, stumbling over the scattered stones and small piles of dirt in the passageway.

Barnett triggered three fast shots after him and he felt a hammer blow in his right side, stumbled to his knees, fell on his side and kept rolling. The wound was still numb and he didn't notice any pain, but when he lunged upright again, outside the cave entrance, he had trouble straightening and his breath was like a knife in his side.

Lewis's shotgun thundered again and he heard the *whrrrruuunppp!* of the heavy, spinning slug passing overhead. He rolled to the slope, sliding part-way on his butt, hurling himself into the bushes as the sixgun crashed again and two bullets clipped branches near his head.

He threw himself forward, made himself get his legs working under him and ran for the picket-line of horses. Barnett was pounding after him, breathing like a locomotive. Lewis was coming, too, crazy hatred driving him on, as he limped and lurched through the brush, panting. He paused, raised the shotgun one-handed, leaning on his crutch for support, and fired. The gun kicked wildly and he almost lost his grip. In the dim light he saw the eruption of gravel two feet from the sprinting, zigzagging Grant as the slug ploughed into the slope.

Grant lost footing ten yards short of the nearest horse, sprawled and skidded, groaning aloud as the wound in his side opened up. He didn't hear any shot, but his left leg kicked violently and he knew another of Barnett's bullets had found him.

He spun away, holding the bleeding wound in the back of his thigh, heaved backwards into the brush and bit down on his lower lip, trying to quieten the involuntary moans that welled up into his throat with a bitter bile.

Barnett, panting, sweating, face full of murder now, slid and stumbled down the slope, smashed into the brush and raised his pistol as he saw Grant.

But Grant had a rock in his hand now and he threw it quickly and with deadly accuracy. Barnett's head jerked back and to one side and the man flung up his arms, went down on one knee, holding his bloody face in his hands.

Grant saw the Colt skidding in the dirt, three yards away. He lunged for it, but his wounds held him back and he desperately dragged himself towards it as Lewis came hobbling up, baring his teeth in a tight grin.

'*Now* I get to blow you apart, Grant!'

He took his time lifting the heavy shotgun, propped it on the edge of the crutch. Grant flung himself forward with a gritted cry of pain, scooped the pistol out of the dirt and twisted on to his back, the world spinning about him as he emptied the Colt into Lewis. The lean man jerked and staggered. The crutch fell, the shotgun following it to the ground. Lewis coughed, clawing at his chest, thudded to his knees, then spread out on his face, one foot drumming briefly.

Barnett lunged for the shotgun, face a mask of blood, got it into his hands and spun towards Grant who held an empty gun in his fist. Grant knew he was a dead man as the shotgun lined-up on his chest....

Then a rifle whip-cracked with a distinctive sound from up the slope and Rafe Barnett's head snapped back violently and the top of his skull was torn off by the bullet. He fell backwards, the unfired shotgun falling across his chest.

Grant stared at the dead man for a moment, then turned his head to look up the slope. He saw nothing. His head was still ringing with the gunfire and the dull roar set up in his ears by his throbbing wounds.

Then a man's shape appeared on his left, approaching silently, dragging one leg a little, one arm tucked into the front of his shirt. His clothes were in rags, as if the man had been crawling through brush or over rough country.

'Judas Priest!' Grant hissed. 'Is that you, Dog?'

There was a grunt and then the wounded Apache staggered into view, but stumbled over the dead Lewis's legs and fell sprawling.

Grant lay back against the slope, an immense weariness overwhelming him suddenly. The world spun about him, faster and faster, until the greyness changed to blackness and he was sucked into the whirlpool that led only to oblivion.

## 8

## Return

Running Dog sat in the leather-sprung chair on the porch of Grant's Busted G ranch house, exercising his healing arm by whittling at a piece of wood. Sweet-smelling cedar shavings piled up about his moccasins and the wolf he was carving gradually took on its shape, little gouges for the hair giving it a more lifelike appearance.

For an Apache with the name of Running Dog, it was a good totem, the wolf being the king of all the dog family.

Now he looked up as he glimpsed a rider coming in across the hard ground, warmed by the early spring sunshine. There was still a bite in the air early morning and evening, but the days were wonderful, clear blue skies, bright sunshine, the sound of birds and the greening creeping across the distant hills. It had been a short but bitter winter and the thaw was causing flood problems in some parts of the valley but the Busted G's creeks and waterholes had filled without flooding.

'Sheriff,' Dog called, without turning his head, lifting his wolf close to his face to work on the eyes.

From inside the house, Grant's voice said, 'Hell, not again! He's been hassling us all damn winter.'

Grant appeared in the doorway, leaning on a stick now, absently massaging the tight skin of the healed bullet wound in his side. He squinted briefly.

'Alone, anyway. Hope you haven't forgot the story, Dog.'

The Apache grunted and threw Grant a contemptuous look. 'My memory OK – not as old as you.'

Grant grinned. 'You sassing me again? Dunno why I keep you around.'

'Need me to save life when you make mistakes.'

Grant sobered slightly, watching Fergus Perry head towards the corrals. 'Yeah. You're handy, I'll give you that.'

He knew he could never forget how Dog had returned for him, one arm torn up by buckshot, his back peppered, a leg hurt from where his pinto had finally gone down under him and crushed it into the rock. He told Grant he'd taken a full day to dig away the ground under his leg so he could pull it free. His fingers were torn badly as he'd had to use his bare hands after his knife blade broke.

Weak from loss of blood, without food, he'd grabbed his Colt revolving rifle and, despite all his awesome dread of the bad-medicine country, had walked for nigh on three days to get to the camp at the mesa and rescue his white man friend.

Not only had he fought down his deep-rooted superstitious fear, but he had travelled at night, something no Apache did unless he really had to. Or wanted to.

But Dog had come and saved him from Barnett.

Both had passed out and, next day when they'd come round and doctored each other some, Grant remembered Ray Sinclair, still trapped in the sinkhole.

They found him at the bottom of the shaft, dead from seven rattlesnake bites. Dog had not been able to conquer his fear enough to descend into the shaft, but he had learned to work the ratchet pulley block quickly and had lowered the wounded Grant down. Bronco had taken Lewis's shotgun, loaded with double-0 buckshot in both barrels, and he'd blasted several rattlers that hissed and struck at him. Ray was long dead, lying in a shallow stream of water that seemed to run right through the tunnel. Bats were plentiful. The stench of their manure and urine was overpowering. He took a quick look inside the tunnel mouth, saw the shattered wagon timbers and more of the gold bars, like the six he had kicked into the shaft last night. He was too weak to even carry one up with him.

But somehow he'd draped Ray over the bosun's chair and Dog had hauled him up. It took a long, long time before the chair came down again and Grant finally returned to the surface. Grant was shaking when he stepped on to solid ground again.

He tried to hide his relief from Dog who watched him closely. He attempted to make a joke out of it. 'See? Back in one piece. No demons down there after all, Dog.'

'Maybe you just didn't see 'em.'

Grant could see what it had cost the Apache to even enter the cave and they lost no time in getting Sinclair's body outside and stretching it out alongside those of Lewis and Barnett. For a time both men collapsed with exhaustion.

Grant fired up his last cheroot and Dog made coffee. They squatted, drinking in silence and then Grant said, 'Helluva lot of gold down that hole, Dog.'

The Indian didn't look at him. 'You want it?'

Grant hesitated. 'Some, I reckon. We've earned it, Dog.'

The Indian shrugged.

'OK, it doesn't interest you and you want to get outa these hills *pronto*. Fine with me. But ... let's get a story straight between us, OK? I mean, we don't have to tell anyone about the mesa or that we were even in this part of the Brimstones, right.'

Running Dog squinted. 'You make story, I go along.'

Grant nodded, thinking hard, not sure yet what he was going to do. In fact, he had kind of surprised himself at the suggestion he had just made. It had come out of nowhere, catching him unawares, but now that he gave it some thought... Well, it had possibilities.

By the time they had finally limped into town, with the dead men draped over the spare horses and mules, Grant had his story set.

They had even picked up an arrow from where they had been attacked by the renegade bucks and Dog had driven it through the centre of Ray Sinclair's chest.

It helped back up their story that they had been attacked by a bunch of drunken bucks on the run from a reservation. But Grant had placed the attack many miles away from the mesa, in fact, on another section of range altogether ... a part known to be frequented by Indians hiding out from the reservation police.

'Kinda stupid goin' into that country, wasn't it, Bronco?' Sheriff Perry had asked.

Grant had shrugged. 'The clients wanted cougar and that's the place to find them.'

'But all you found was Injuns, huh?'

Grant met and held the lawman's stare. 'That's right. First clients I've ever lost. Can't see it doing my hunting reputation much good.'

'No. Well, I guess it's straightforward enough. You aren't the first whites to be attacked by them goddamn Apaches.' Perry flicked his gaze to the silent Running Dog but nothing changed in Dog's flat face. 'That young feller would've died anyways, from them snakebites. How come none of 'em had been treated, Bronco?'

Just like Perry, trying to blind-side him, thought Grant. The man looked fat and he was sure lazy, but he had a lawman's suspicious mind and he was pretty damn good at interrogation.

'He got bit while he was taking cover from the Indians,' Grant explained. 'We heard him yelling but no one had time to see what was wrong at that stage. Next, we found he'd taken an arrow through the heart and then we saw all those snakebites. Way too late to do anything then.'

Perry wrote it all down, made them sign copies, before he would even allow them to see the doctor for treatment of their own wounds...

That was nearly four months ago and it had been a slow recovery during the winter. Both Grant and Running Dog were just starting to get on top again now and Grant had hinted once or twice that maybe they should take a trip up into the Brimstones again, check out the mesa, see if the spring run-off had affected the tunnel where the gold was.

'We can build this place up the way I've always wanted to, Dog, with some of that gold.'

Dog grunted. 'Perry will want to know where you get money.'

Grant frowned, nodding. 'Yeah, I know. I'm working on that part.'

And now here was Fergus Perry dismounting in his ranch yard, wiping sweat from his moon face, waddling up towards the house.

''Mornin', gents. Gonna be a long hot summer if this early spring's anythin' to go by.'

'Could be right, Fergus. Got no lemonade but there's a pot of java on the kitchen range.'

Perry paused with one foot on the bottom

step, screwing up his face. 'Got somethin' to put in it, give a man a little boost? It sure is a long ride out from town...'

Grant smiled thinly. 'Reckon I can find a coupla fingers of rye. Come on in, Fergus.' As he stood aside, the perspiring lawman stepped past him, Grant's nose wrinkling at the sour smell of the man's clothes. He asked casually, 'What brings you all the way out here ... again?'

Perry told him over coffee in the kitchen. Dog sat at one end of the deal table, sipping from his chipped cup, mostly silent as usual.

'This ain't the only long ride I've took lately,' the sheriff said, sniffing the rye in his coffee as the fumes rose with the heat. 'Been out into the Brimstones.' He looked up and set his gaze on Grant's puzzled face. 'Still a little snow on the high peaks, lots of flooded washes from the run-off, but I reckon I found that place where you claimed you was attacked.'

'Where we *were* attacked, Fergus.'

The sheriff nodded. 'Yeah, well, you know,

I couldn't find much evidence of any sort of battle like you described, Bronco. No empty shells or spent arrows, dropped tomahawks. No bloodstains, though I din' hold out much hope of findin' *them* after the snows. But, maybe I had the wrong place, huh?'

Grant spoke carefully, holding his mug in both hands. 'Reckon you must've.'

'Apaches take dead for burial,' Dog spoke up suddenly. 'No leave weapons.'

The look Perry shot the Indian was hostile but he scratched at his head and spoke civilly enough. 'Yeah, I guess you're right, Dog, but I'd still've expected to find spent shells if the fight was as fierce as Bronco says.'

'You didn't have the right place, Fergus. That's the only explanation.'

Perry nodded gently. 'Uh-huh. You fit enough to take me out and *show* me the right place?'

Grant stiffened. 'The hell for?'

'Have to get my report all correct, and I really oughta see where it happened. Didn't

164

press you when the snows came because you wasn't fit enough. But now...'

Grant's eyes narrowed. 'Someone riding you over this, Fergus?'

The lawman was silent for a long time, drank half his coffee, reached for the whiskey bottle and filled the cup again. 'Matter of fact, yeah. The Denver marshal. Seems this Barnett and Lewis worked for Adam Fellows...'

Grant fought to keep his face blank. 'And who's he?'

'Big businessman in Denver. Owns several saloons, freight, warehouses, coupla stores. You know – important. He's the one wants to make sure all this is above board.' Perry held up a hand as Grant started to bristle. 'Simmer down, Bronco. The Denver marshal's gettin' his butt burned and he's passin' it along to me. I gotta see where the fight happened. I've already told him you've got a good reputation and so on and likely he's happy enough with that, but this Fellows wants the follow-through.'

Grant sighed and shrugged. 'Haven't sat a horse all winter, Fergus. Dunno if I could manage a long ride straight-off. Gimme a coupla days to get in shape and I'll take you to where we were attacked.'

'Well, that's good enough for me. Oh, one more thing: Fellows claims Barnett had some kind of map to a special area he wanted to go. He was to check out a possible freight route for Fellows, cut some miles off his Salt Lake City run – know anythin' about that?'

Grant shook his head slowly. 'Never mentioned it. He and Lewis only talked hunting. They got a couple of elk stags, missed some bighorn sheep and then set their hearts on cougar. I didn't go through their things, though.'

Perry seemed surprised. 'Reckon I would've.'

'Well, Fergus, we were both wounded, we had three dead men on our hands and weren't sure if the Apaches were coming back or not. We just got out of there as well

166

as we could.'

'I guess that makes sense. OK, Bronco. You come into town two days from now and we'll ride up into the hills and see if you can locate this place where you was attacked.'

After he'd gone, Grant turned slowly to Dog. 'He's sniffing around for something.'

'Maybe map. Could be he knows what it is.'

'Well, that's one thing he won't find – I burned it. We don't need it and I figured if it was found it'd take some explaining away. Burned Barnett's journal, too.'

Dog nodded approval. 'You take sheriff to where we were attacked on way in, he wonder how come you weren't further into hills after a week on the trail.'

Grant smiled. 'I'll tell him we were doubling back to get up into cougar country.'

But it wasn't that easy. Perry wanted to see other places where they had camped and hunted. Grant was sure Perry suspected something, smelled some money in this somewhere, or he knew more than he was telling. But after almost a full day in the Brimstones he claimed he was satisfied and would wire the Denver marshal to that effect.

'What you gonna do now, Bronco? You got no stock to speak of and by the time you do get some, the army'll have bought all they want for their summer campaigns.'

'Got no choice but to try and catch some mustangs and get them broke enough before the army stops buying, Fergus, no other choice at all.'

Perry nodded slowly, studying Grant's face with its new scars. 'You'll be coming back into the Brimstones, then?'

'When Dog and me're fit enough. I tell you, Fergus, I'm about plumb tuckered after just riding in here with you. Couldn't hope to build traps and start busting broncs yet a spell.'

'Well, I wish you luck. I'll head on back to town. Obliged for your help, Bronco.'

Grant watched the fat sheriff take the trail

to Brimstone and then set his mount slowly forward down the slope towards the barely discernible trail that would lead him back to his spread. Dog followed silently, but after an hour's ride, said, 'Sheriff smell something.'

'Yeah, wouldn't mind betting he searches the ranch after we head for the hills.'

'You go after gold?'

Grant hitched around in the saddle. 'Have to, Dog. Perry's right about the army. We ain't gonna have enough of a string to offer them for sale before they quit buying summer stock. We're broke, and the only place I know where I can lay my hands on some cash is that mesa. Will you come back with me? I know it's a lot to ask but, well, you seen there's nothing to be afraid of. No demons or stuff, I mean.'

Dog hesitated. They descended to the next section of trail before he answered.

'I come.'

Grant nodded soberly but when he turned back to the trail, he smiled slowly.

*Now* he felt better.

Or he did until he returned to the ranch and found the girl waiting for him.

'Hello,' she called, standing up from where she had been sitting in the leather-slung porch chair 'You must be Mr Grant and Running Dog–' She stepped into the sunlight and her hair was suddenly burnished a deep red-gold. The smile tightened a trifle as she said, 'I'm Donna Ferris. The one who set up Ray Sinclair for a fleecing by Fellows' gamblers in Denver. I'm sure he would've mentioned me.'

## 9

## Buckskin Girl

She was about the same age as Ray Sinclair had been, maybe a year or two younger. She was dressed in a fringed buckskin jacket over a white cotton blouse, tucked into the waistband of light-coloured corduroy trousers. Her half boots were soft buckskin, also fringed around the tops, matching the jacket. A small, narrow-brimmed hat hung down her back by its plaited tie-thong.

She had a sunburned look, had not yet tanned, and she favoured gloves, likely to protect her small hands. Her eyes were clear and grey-green and steady, her nose a mite sharp, her mouth small but looking as if it smiled a good deal.

And as she came down the steps to meet

the weary men, Grant noticed that the smile, tentative as it was, touched her eyes. She held up her right hand.

'You are Bronco Grant...?'

He took the hand and shook briefly as he nodded. Her grip was firm enough. 'I am. This is my pard, Running Dog.'

'Known generally as "Dog", I believe,' she said, smiling as she turned and offered the Apache her hand also.

He grunted as he shook once and released her.

'How d'you know so much about us, Miss Ferris?' Grant asked.

'Ray wrote to me, said he was waiting in Brimstone to be met by Dog. He'd heard a good deal about you.'

'From Fellows?'

She held Grant's steady gaze and nodded gently. 'I expect so.'

'You still work for Adam Fellows?'

Donna Ferris took a deep breath and sighed. 'No. That was a–a desperate time. I was stranded in Denver. I'd had my money stolen through my own stupidity. Apparently it happens to a lot of naïve people, of both sexes, because there was a woman came to see me within hours of my loss, offering me a job. She obviously expected me to be in desperate straits.'

Grant nodded. 'I've heard of such things. And you took the job she offered?'

He was surprised to see her blush and she lowered her eyes, shaking her head vigorously. 'No, it-it was not to my liking.'

Suddenly he savvied and he half-smiled as he asked, 'Dancehall gal?'

Her eyes flashed. 'For want of a better name!' Then her mouth softened. 'So she offered me an alternative: I could entice men to drink or gamble and I'd be paid a percentage of what they spent in her saloon.'

'What they call a "shill".'

'Don't sound so superior! It's *very* different for a girl from St Louis, alone and friendless in a frontier town – which is all Denver is – than it is for a man in the same situation!'

'Yeah, I guess it is, ma'am. Ray told us you set him up for a fleecing.'

Her gaze wavered again and he saw the flash of shame in her eyes. 'Yes ... I knew what they were doing, but he was boasting how much money he had, was throwing it around to impress people. Unfortunately, it was only talk and he lost much more than he could afford.'

'Then they beat him and stole ... something ... from him which they decided could be used to pay his debt.'

'No!' Her sharp denial startled Grant and even Dog frowned at her vehemence. 'It was *my* map! Ray did the stealing! He was desperate, I suppose. I took him in after they'd beaten him and given him twenty-four hours to find the money or – well, you know the kind of threats gamblers make.'

Grant frowned. 'He told us a story about that map, how his uncle had been one of the escort of the wagons that had been swallowed by a sinkhole in '64.'

Donna smiled crookedly. '*My* Uncle Ned!

No doubt the rest of the story was true enough, except it wasn't Ray's kin, but mine. I felt guilty about setting him up. I told him the only thing I had that *might* be of value was the old map and I told him how I came by it. He said Barnett wouldn't be interested in anything like that, but when I woke up next morning, he'd gone. So had my map and some loose change I'd left on the table...'

Grant was silent a spell then said slowly, 'Miss, I'm not doubting you, but Ray didn't strike me as being that kind of man.'

'No, of course not.' Her smile was warm, a mite pensive, no doubt as she remembered her time with young Sinclair. 'I think he was basically decent, a bit of a show-off, and certainly a womanizer. But he was really scared of Lewis and Barnett. I didn't really blame him and, well, he did take time to write to me from Brimstone and apologize and tell me he had traded the map and his caving expertise for the cancelling of his gambling debts.' She shrugged. 'I was working in a store in Denver by that time, hoping to save enough to return to St Louis. Then I heard the news that Ray was dead, along with the others. Denver was snowed-in most of the winter as you no doubt know and I finally had enough money to catch a train to Brimstone, hire a horse and come to see you.'

Grant and Dog exchanged glances but the Indian's was unreadable. Grant seemed puzzled and uncomfortable. 'Why did you want to see me, Miss Ferris?'

'Call me "Donna", please. Why, I wanted to know if you'd located the mesa and if the gold really was there – and, if it was, of course, to claim what is, after all rightfully mine. Surely, you can't have any argument with that, Mr Grant?'

They sat at the supper-table over the remains of the meal that Donna Ferris had made. Both men agreed that she was a fine cook.

Grant sat back in his chair, lit a cheroot,

looking at the girl through the first exhalation of smoke as he waved out the match flame.

'Been thinking about what you said, Donna, about the gold being yours.'

Her face sharpened. 'It is! If it's there – and I must say you've carefully avoided telling me one way or the other, Bronco!'

He nodded. 'It's there, all right. I've seen it.'

Donna leaned towards him across the table. 'Lord! it really is true?' At his nod she smiled and clapped her small hands together once. 'I can't believe it! That old map has been floating around our family for years. No one really believed the story about Uncle Ned. He always exaggerated things, but I-I had this *feeling* that it would be too much to believe he would attempt one of his famous jokes on his deathbed. When I decided to come West, I brought the map with me and I suppose I had the intention of somehow checking it out, perhaps searching for the mesa, but I never expected things to happen the way they have.'

Grant was silent. Dog just sat there, perfectly still, face blank, sprawled at his ease in the chair as if he was a world away in his thoughts, far removed from the conversation taking place.

The girl had sobered now. 'You don't think I have a claim on that gold, do you?'

'Well, strictly speaking, it belongs to the Confederacy which, no longer in existence, I guess makes that gold up for grabs.'

Their gazes locked and after a time, breathing a little faster, she said, 'To whoever finds it first? Is that what you're saying?' He nodded slowly, and her mouth tightened. 'Which means you!'

Again he nodded, but swiftly held up a hand as she began to protest. 'I led Lewis and Barnett to the mesa. Ray was the one went down blind into that hellhole. Dog and me both had to fight for our lives and so I reckon we've got a damn good claim to that gold.'

'Meaning I've done nothing! Damn you,

Bronco Grant, you don't understand what ... hell ... I've been through to get here.' She slapped a hand against the table and Dog slid his dark eyes around to her. 'I–I had a very *proper* upbringing. We had a maid and a cook. My family died and left debts and I've been working to try and pay them off. I'm out of my depth in this situation ... I make all kinds of foolish mistakes, like allowing what money I had to be stolen. I've been frightened out of my wits most of the time. I've had drunks trying to get into my bed. I was beaten once and saved from very serious assault only because a deputy happened along in the nick of time. So, Mr Bronco Grant, don't tell me about the hardships you've faced getting to that gold because that won't wash with me. What I've been through in the light of my background, was, to me, every bit as bad as anything you and Running Dog and even Ray, faced!'

Her rounded bosom was heaving now and her breath came in short gasps with her emotion. Her eyes were bright and glittering and her head was held high and straight and proud. Grant almost smiled at the picture: this slim young girl, no more than five-feet six in her half-boots, ready to take on the whole damn world.

Now her eyes darted from Grant to Dog and back again. 'I see that what I've just told you hasn't had much effect so I must tell you something else; if you *don't* take me to this mesa, I'll cut off my nose to spite my face and tell my story in Brimstone to anyone who'll listen.'

That made Grant sit up straighter. 'If you can't have the gold, no one does, right?'

'Not at all, Bronco. If I can't have it, *everyone* can have a share. And yours will be a very small one in that case I would think.'

'And your own?' he asked tightly.

She shrugged. 'It was all just a dream. I never really expected it to come true ... I'll be very little worse off. In fact, I could even come out of it better than you – if I find someone with a sense of fairness to talk to.'

He waved smoke away from his face with

a tired gesture. 'Hell, Ray said there were millions in gold down in that hole. I saw some of it, was too weak to bring up a bar or two – wanted to get Ray out of that place. But there's plenty to go round. I guess I was just riled the way you slapped your brand on it right away...'

Her smile was a trifle stiff at the edges. 'I was willing to share it with you, still am, I don't expect to have your services for nothing. I was thinking of a fifty-fifty split.'

Grant felt ashamed. He had misjudged her and he felt mad at himself for exhibiting greedy tendencies the way he had. Dog hadn't approved, but had held his peace, even though it was all there in his eyes for those who could read the Indian a little. Now Dog stared and his gaze told Grant that he was waiting for his reply.

Grant sighed, smiled, thrust his hand across the table. 'Deal, Donna.'

She smiled widely as she shook his hand. 'You're taking my story on trust?'

'Somehow it makes more sense than

Ray's, although the way he told it it seemed pretty good. But it'll be in your own interest to say nothing. I'll spread the word that you're kin from back East, looking after this place while Dog and me're up in the hills trying to trap mustangs.'

Her smile vanished and she stood swiftly. 'You'll do nothing of the sort! I intend to come with you and help raise every bar of gold that's possible! And if you think any different, Bronco Grant, you've got another think coming!'

Grant was surprised to see what could have been the beginnings of a smile on Dog's usually impassive face.

He threw up his arms. 'Hell!' he said feelingly.

Sheriff Fergus Perry looked up as a shadow darkened the door of his office and a wide-shouldered man edged in, followed by two more.

Perry set down the pen he had been using, let his right hand drop below his desk level, close to the butt of the sawn-off shotgun he had slung there on leather straps, the shortened muzzles pointing towards the thin plywood that covered in the front of the desk well.

'Howdy, Sheriff,' the first man said warmly enough. 'Remember me?'

The man moved slightly so the bright sunlight wasn't behind him and Perry slid his gaze that way, but at the same time checked out the other two.

They were hardcases, trail-stained, everready for trouble. He'd seen a thousand just like them. So he switched his gaze back to the wide-shouldered man and gave a small start.

'You're ... Chuck? No, Chick! The one got beatup by Bronco Grant last Fall, right outside there on the street.'

Chick smiled thinly through his stubble. 'Got a good memory for faces, Sheriff.'

'Hell, won't forget you in a hurry. That was some fight. And I've never been able to figure out how come you quit town the next day lookin' so happy about it with your face banged-up the way it was.'

Chick shrugged again. 'Happy-go-lucky, that's me. No, I was paid to pick a fight with Grant, test him, see if he was tough as folk made out.'

Perry's jaw dropped an inch. 'I ... don't get it.'

'Never mind about it now. It's done. We know how tough Grant is – I mean he managed to kill two of Mr Fellows' top guns – and fool you and everyone else into believin' it was Injuns done it.'

Perry's jaw dropped another inch. 'The hell d'you know about it?'

'More than you, Sheriff. Look, I'm representing Mr Fellows. He read your report, passed along by the Denver marshal and he said to tell you you done pretty good, but he just don't believe it, is all.'

Fergus Perry flushed, half rose. 'Now wait a minute! I'm a professional, mister, and no one – Adam Fellows or no one else – calls me a liar or tells me I've done sloppy work.'

'Take it easy, Perry,' said one of the hardcases, a man with a jet-black beard and shoulder-length hair of the same colour. His right hand was resting casually on his gun butt and the lawman, who had relinquished his own hold on the sawn-off shotgun, suddenly realized he was at a mighty awkward disadvantage.

These men looked like killers, of a sudden, and that included the apparently good-natured 'Chick'.

Sheriff Perry eased back gently in his chair, careful to keep his hands in plain sight. He made his eyes hard as he looked from one man to the other,

'I don't savvy why you gents are here.'

'Hey, you ain't been listenin', Sheriff,' Chick said, half-smiling. 'Mr Fellows ain't satisfied about the way Harve Lewis and Rafe Barnett died. He sent me up to make my own investigation.'

'Now, you wait up! *I've* investigated and I'm satisfied Grant's story's true. No reason for him to make it up, in any case, and I don't let amateurs into my bailiwick, goin' over ground I've already covered.'

Chick sighed, glanced at the black-bearded man and his companion, who looked part-Mexican.

'Well, they did say he weren't too bright.'

'By God, mister...'

'Siddown!' This time the gun was already in the bearded man's hand and the hammer was cocked back under his thumb. The breed had one of his twin pistols out, too, but hadn't yet cocked it: his thumb rested on the hammer spur, though.

Perry felt the sweat prickle his skin and slide down over his rolls of fat under his arms and around his midriff.

'Maybe ... maybe if you explained a little more...? Then I could likely be of some help to you gents?' His voice suddenly hardened. 'But I sure as hell don't take to strangers bustin' into my office and pulling a gun on me!'

'Just one of the things you'd best get used to, Sheriff,' Chick told him, kicking out a chair and dropping into it. He took out the makings, casually began to build a cigarette.

Perry showed no signs of fear as he watched the men confronting him. 'What you mean "get used to"?'

Chick licked the paper and winked. 'Mr Fellows wants to put you on the payroll, Sheriff. Then you can't complain we're strangers doin' anythin' to you. Smart man, Mr Fellows. Knows how to get what he wants.' He leaned forward abruptly and scraped a vesta across Perry's leather vest, lighting up and blowing smoke into the surprised lawman's face. 'Pays right well, too. You in, Sher'f? Or you out? And "out" in this case means *permanently*, you know what I mean?'

## 10

## Hellhole

Grant could see Dog growing more tense as they approached the mesa. There was little enough showing, but he had known the man for many years, lived close with him, knew all his small mannerisms and the signs were there.

He was tightening up the nearer they came to the mesa and Hell's Doorway.

Grant still marvelled that the man had come back for him that other time, into country that held such fear and dread. He didn't laugh at the Apache's beliefs: a man was entitled to believe in his own gods – or devils. And he knew how they could drive some men out of their heads, send them plumb loco, turn them into jibbering idiots

188

so that they ran screaming into the night.

Running Dog was stronger than that but the terror had been bred into him by the tribal shaman into *all* of the tribe.

Grant respected Dog's beliefs and now he dropped back on the trail, the girl half turning in her saddle to watch as he drew up alongside the Apache who was leading the pack mules.

'Dog, you don't have to do this.'

Dog's gaze was impassive. 'You wrong, Bronco. I *have* to do this.'

Grant started to speak again and then cut off the words abruptly. He nodded in understanding.

Dog had done it before, driven by loyalty to Grant, a loyalty so strong it had overridden his long-held terror of Hell's Doorway. He had had little time to think, had concentrated on getting there in time to save Grant's life, the will to travel without food and water, wounded as he was, pushing those fears to the back of his mind.

This time he was going in cold and it was

harder, much harder. But he had done it once and he knew if he did it again he would be over that long-held fear. Unless, of course, there *were* demons lurking that hadn't yet appeared...

*That* was how the Apache thought: unable to entirely shake all the old superstition – and Grant was one of the few white men who could savvy – and respect this thing.

He leaned from the saddle and slapped Dog's leg lightly. 'OK, *amigo*. See you later. I'm gonna do a little scouting and check things out.'

Donna swung around at his words, mildly alarmed.

Dog lifted a hand silently. The girl called to Grant as he veered away.

'Where're you going?'

'Scouting.' He began to rein his horse around.

'You're going the wrong way! We've just come that way.

The girl was more alert than he'd thought. 'Old army habit: always check your backtrail before scouting ahead. Danger can come from either direction. You'll be all right with Dog.'

Donna turned her smile on the sad-looking Indian. 'Yes, I know.'

Grant lifted a hand and headed back across the country they had travelled earlier.

That night they kept the camp-fire small and Dog stayed close to the flames, the broken mesa rearing over them against the stars. He sipped coffee from a battered mug and spoke softly without looking at Grant while the girl gathered the supper dishes.

'Backtrail clear?'

Donna frowned at Grant. 'Surely you would've told us by now if it wasn't!'

Grant hesitated. 'No sense in alarming everyone unnecessarily.'

She stiffened, face sharpening. 'You saw something!'

'Not really. Likely a dust devil. Just a glimpse of it in a canyon but it didn't reappear.'

'Best stand guard tonight,' Dog said flatly

and Grant admired the man for suggesting such a thing.

'I'm not tired. I can do it,' Grant said casually.

Dog stared over his coffee mug. 'I take turn.' It was said flatly and there was a menace in there that said 'And don't forget to wake me!' Grant nodded and was surprised when the girl insisted on taking a stint, too.

She was a gutsy little lady, all right.

The frame still stood, the ropes and bosun's chair and ratchet pulleys dangling just as he had last seen them except for the thin covering of bat excreta here and there. The sinkhole and the cave had the same stench, too, and the blazing torches they took with them sent bats on the arched roof of the cave screaming and beating their wings, finally surging around wildly, bringing a few startled cries from the girl.

But she was standing up better than Grant had expected, a mighty game little thing and not afraid of work, even if she had been used to servants doing things for her in her earlier years: seemed she'd been self-sufficient for a long time. Dog was silent most of the time, and he was taking much care now in hiding his feelings, not wanting Grant to pick up on them. Grant admired the Apache, knowing what it must be costing him.

He should have found some way to keep Dog away from the mesa but he knew even as he had the thought that he would never have been able to do it. Dog was in on this deal and he was going to see it through.

So Grant figured to just quit worrying about it: the Apache was strong enough to fight his own battles, mental or physical. What they had to do now was concentrate on bringing up that gold – and the first thing they had to do was find out the conditions at the bottom of the hellhole.

He knew that was his job and he prepared for it right away ... and not with any great deal of eagerness.

It was an offer too good to refuse.

Perry was stunned by the amount the mysterious and powerful Adam Fellows was offering for his services, cash up front, too. Chick Mundy had an authority to draw the cash from the Brimstone First National and he sent the breed, Mexican Jack, across the street to get it after the sheriff had agreed to Fellows' terms.

Out of the generous amount, though, Perry had to provide two more men who would do the job required of them and keep their mouths shut. He was also responsible for hiring packmules.

Perry sighed, arranged it with the livery man and then went back to the cellblock at the law office and looked at the two sick-and-sorry men snoring on the reeking bunks. He ran his bunch of keys back and forth across the bars until they groaned and complained and sat up, holding their heads, cussing him out good.

'Shut up or I'll give you time on the chain gang,' Perry threatened: he had four prisoners already under a deputy's guard repairing the bridge at the end of Main where it had been damaged by the floods caused by the rapid thaw. He looked at these two hardcases, though they seemed anything but hard right now.

Brawlers, petty thieves, stand-over types – they had been a thorn in his side for years. He suspected Monaghan had killed a couple of drunks when he was desperate for money, but had never been able to prove anything. The other one, smaller, rat-cunning, called himself Mailer though Perry knew it wasn't his real name. He had used these two for a couple of under-the-table jobs from time to time. They were easy to blackmail and if you spelled out everything for them they were even halfway reliable. And they knew the Brimstones pretty good, had hid out there more than once.

But in this case, their talent for violence without remorse was what he wanted. He unlocked the cell door and they froze, squinting, knowing they had another four days of their sentence yet to serve.

'Go get cleaned up. We're goin' for a little ride. No questions asked and fifty bucks apiece guaranteed.'

That was all there was to it.

Not that Chick Mundy thought they were a good choice, but it didn't really matter: they wouldn't be coming back. Nor would Perry. But for now he had use for all of them.

'You know these Brimstones pretty good, Perry, want you to take us to a broken mesa that someone named Hell's Doorway. Here, I've a copy of the original map. Know it?'

Perry didn't even look at the creased map. 'That's a ways!'

Chick sighed. 'Perry, you been paid and paid good. From here on in, you don't argue, and you don't get uppity and you sure as hell don't never flash your goddamn badge at me! Savvy?' Perry flushed but said nothing, Chick leaned closer, 'You ... do ... what ... I say! Pronto! You been bought, mister, just like them two sorry-lookin' bar rats you hired. Now, look at the map and take me to that mesa!'

Perry didn't like it but he tightened his mouth and nodded curtly. He guessed he could swallow the kind of treatment he knew he was going to get from now on for $500. He took the crude map, sighing.

'I don't know the way any too well. Feller who knows the Brimstones best round these parts is–'

'Bronco Grant, yeah we know that. Judas, Perry, you're dumber than I figured. It's Grant we're followin'! But he ain't gonna leave tracks for us. So you gotta get us to this mesa quick-smart.'

Perry frowned. 'How you know Grant's gone there?'

Mundy looked as if he would hit the sheriff but controlled himself. He spoke between his teeth. 'Because I've had a man watchin' his place ever since that gal arrived. Christ! Don't ask me which gal! Just, for hell's sakes, *do like I say!*'

Perry nodded. 'Don't blame me if we get lost.'

'Perry, I *will* blame you! So don't get lost!'

Chick shook his head at Blackie and Mexican Jack, plainly exasperated.

Fergus Perry glowered at Monaghan and Mailer, just daring them to snigger, then he spurred his mount forward and led the group into the foothills of the Brimstones.

Grant didn't really recall much of his descent into the sinkhole before when he had been wounded and went down to check on Ray Sinclair sprawled at the bottom of the shaft.

That time was little more than a blur in his memory now.

He dropped down in jerks, carrying a blazing torch of tightly wrapped rags soaked in coal-oil, the flames painting crumbling walls with eerie shadows and movement. He had a shotgun slung to one side of the chair and spare shells in his pockets. He knew there would still be snakes and he figured the combination of fire and buckshot ought to clear them away.

He was a mite leery of doing too much shooting down below. He didn't recall much about the tunnel except it seemed high enough for a man to stand in and was dripping droplets of crystal clear water – rain that had fallen years ago, according to Ray, slowly filtering down through sand and limestone, likely the purest water any man would ever drink in this lifetime.

As Grant's boots touched bottom, soggy and spongy, he waved the blazing torch around. It *whooshed!*, the flames dragging small trails through the air, and he saw shadows move. At ground level. Which meant snakes. Hundreds of eyes glowed in the dark of the tunnel as the flickering light whipped by and he heard the stirring of the bats. There was a flapping sound and he held the torch down, saw a small bat had apparently fallen and been pounced on by a snake that was devouring it.

He swallowed. He *hated* snakes and here he was going to have to work knee-deep amongst them.

But that other glow, the glitter that jumped back at him from here and there on the tunnel floor – that would make the risk worth while.

It came from the scattered bars of gold.

Walking gingerly – he recalled how Ray had said these sinkholes often didn't have a solid bottom, only a kind of debris-built platform at intervals and which could give way under a man at any time – he looped a rope under his arms and it was Donna's job up top to pay it out or haul it in taut as he moved about.

He lit the second torch he had brought down, jammed its butt into spongy earth on one wall. The flames flickered and made a quiet hissing sound. He felt the air current against his sweating face and wondered just where it was coming from – somewhere way beyond the darkness that began at the edge of light cast by the torches. Snakes rattled warningly. He blasted with the shotgun. He was almost deafened and the gunsmoke wreathed him, making him cough. He fired both barrels, standing at the beginning of the tunnel where the piled debris of the shattered wagons was.

Through the ringing in his ears he vaguely heard the girl calling down the shaft to know if everything was all right.

'Snakes!' he bawled, wondering if she would hear or if the word would be lost somewhere in the shaft. The top was a ragged dim circle far above. He could just make out the shape of the girl who must be leaning over the edge to call down.

There were seven writhing snakes and others slithered away into holes and hiding places as he reloaded, heaved some rocks and rotting wood aside, exposing a nest of the reptiles, all entwined and slithering and oily in the flickering light. He blasted most of them into raw meat, used the smoking barrels to heave aside more of the wood, exposing more rattlers. The air was warm down here which likely accounted for their activity. Three more charges and he had almost thirty snakes dead or dying – and he knew there were still more, but hopefully they would stay hidden now after seeing what had happened to their brethren.

He sure as hell hoped so, because dirt and loose stones had started dropping down on his shoulders after firing the last two loads.

The concussion was loosening something and he had no wish to die down here away from the sunlight, amongst Dog's demons... *Whoa! Quit thinking that way!*

He was already breathing faster than normal and when he became aware of it, made a conscious effort to drag down slow, regular breaths. He felt his hammering heart steady down, wishing he had thought to bring a pair of leather shotgun chaps in case in the dark he inadvertently stood on a snake.

He had heaved the shattered wood into a pile and, throat dry, began looking around, burning torch in one hand, shotgun in the other. There was the gold, spilled out of the rotted false bottoms of the two wagons. The horses' skeletons housed snakes, their gleaming bodies sliding out of the empty eye sockets and open mouths. A charge of buckshot had shattered one of the skulls to splinters.

Rusted percussion arms from the Civil War were scattered all over the place, some still loaded, a couple with ramrods in the barrels. There was gunpowder spilling from broken kegs, embossed copper and brass powder flasks mixed with the gold bars, lead Minie balls for the muskets, oxidized and verdigrised cartridges for the old Henrys and Spencer carbines.

And there were the skeletons of men, the bones long since scattered and broken by whatever animals prowled through this old underground river course. He had strained to listen for a flow of water but there was only the drip-drip-drip from the limestone roof. Apparently the big thaw hadn't sent extra water down these tunnels, which suited him just fine. He had enough to contend with now without the threat of a flash flood as well.

The torch was dying. He went back to the bottom of the shaft, striking his head once on a low part of the tunnel. While he had been exploring, Dog and the girl had lowered down a box containing half-a-dozen oil lamps and some old meat hooks, straightened on one end. He hammered these into the limestone with his gun butt, lit the lanterns and swung them from the hooks. They cast a dull ruddy glow over the area where he figured to be working.

Drawing on heavy leather gloves which he took from his belt, he noted how wet his shirt was – more with sweat than from the drips of water from the tunnel roof, he figured.

He found he was mouth-breathing, edgy, jumping at every sound, lifting his boots quickly as shadows moved on the ground. The bats were shrilling and he saw three more snakes, one as thick as his forearm. That did it.

He touched the blazing torch to the pile of wagon wood and it flared up, most of it dry, though rotted. Flames crackled and heat slapped at his face and bats squealed and flew madly about him. He beat them away from his face, choking in the smoke, stumbling out into the bottom of the shaft. He got his feet into the slack canvas of the bosun's chair and jerked the rope three times, hard...

He was lifted almost immediately, rising in jerky sections, coughing, eyes streaming as the smoke from his fire surged up with the draught. Heat singed him, snatched his breath.

He was gasping and racked by violent coughing fits when hands pulled him sprawling on his face into the cavern.

He couldn't speak and Dog got him out into the sunlight. He sloshed canteen water over his face and singed hair, swilled out his mouth, bathed his eyes and drank.

By that time the smoke pouring out of the cave had stopped, rising lazily into the brilliant sunshine against the cloudless blue of the Colorado sky.

'Figured if I burned the wagon wood it'd drive out the bats *and* the snakes,' Grant explained. 'There's powder down there but too old and wet to explode, might burn though.'

'Might work,' conceded Dog, that new tautness about his mouth since he had returned to the mesa.

'The gold is there?' Donna asked tautly.

Grant smiled, reached inside his shirt and dumped a mud-streaked gold bar on to the ground.

It was blinding where the metal caught the sunlight, dazzling all three of them...

On a high ridge, three or four back from where the mesa began, Fergus Perry stood with one foot up on a boulder while he slowly raked the sun-hammered country with a pair of field glasses.

Then Perry stiffened, adjusted focus slightly and yelled, 'Hey! I see smoke! A lot of it! There, away to the west!'

'There don't look to be many trees out

that way so likely ain't a forest fire...' opined Chick climbing up beside the sheriff and reaching for the glasses. 'Camp-fire?'

'Too big. Dunno what it might be but I'll bet my life it's got somethin' to do with Grant.'

Chick lowered the glasses and looked soberly at the lawman. 'That's exactly what you're doin', Perry, bettin' your life. Now, let's get going and see if we can check it out by sundown.'

'Hell, we won't get across all them ridges by sundown! Might make it by noon tomorrow...'

Chick Mundy turned as he clambered down, his voice cold.

'We travel all night then. But I aim to be where that smoke's coming from by sun-up, latest. So move your fat ass, Perry! Start earnin' that money you been paid!'

**11**

## Out of Hell

Grant's muscles were stiff next morning and his chest and throat felt raw from the smoke he had inhaled. Dog was already up – Grant suspected the Apache hadn't slept much, if at all, camped as they were just outside the entrance to the cavern.

The girl awoke within minutes of Dog starting the breakfast fire, smiled sleepily at the men and made her way down to the small creek.

'Think we might rip up some of that brush on the slope and toss it down the shaft, Dog. There're more snakes down there than mosquitoes in a Louisiana swamp. If they're gonna give me more trouble, I want fire down there, lots of it. The shotgun explosions seem to be weakening parts of the roof, anyway.'

'I cut brush while you eat.'

'How about you?'

'Not hungry.'

Grant watched thoughtfully as the Apache took his tomahawk and moved towards the brush-clad slope. Donna returned, her hair wet, looking after the Indian. Grant told her where he was going.

'Has he eaten already?'

'No, and I don't think he will. Reckon this mesa is getting to him a lot more than he's letting on. He's fighting hard but – look, sooner we get the gold up, the sooner we can all get out of here.'

Donna nodded slowly. 'You care a great deal for him, don't you?'

'We been pards a long time,' he told her simply.

He ate swiftly, though lingered over his coffee while he smoked a cheroot, hearing the rhythmic thuds of Dog's axe on the slope. The girl ate in silence. It was just one more thing Grant liked about her – she didn't talk simply for the sake of talking.

He felt her eyes on him and looked up, mildly startled. She smiled faintly and said, 'We don't need all the gold, Bronco. I mean, a single bar at the price they're paying in Creede and Denver is worth several thousand dollars. Two or three would make me happy. I'd have enough to pay off the debts my parents left me with and there'd be plenty left over to start up some sort of small business.'

Grant watched her face and slowly nodded as he gave her a wide, warm smile. He was thinking it was mighty nice to be partners with someone who wasn't greed-blinded by gold...

'You put it that way, a couple or three bars would suit Dog and me, too. We could get our spread fixed-up, do it slow and easy so as not to raise too many eyebrows. Maybe later ... it's not quite enough...'

His voice trailed off and she said quietly, 'You could tap into the remainder at some future date if you needed to.' After a hesitation he nodded.

'Well, as long as it's just lying there...'

'Of course. I would probably want to do the same. But for now – why don't we set a limit of raising, say, ten bars? Then we could be away from here late today and Dog could begin to relax again.'

Grant thought he loved her in that moment: she was willing to settle for a small part of the gold just so that Running Dog could get away from this devil country and shake some of the terrible fears he was fighting so valiantly. Yes! This was one fine woman, this Donna Ferris, Grant allowed.

Everything went along fine until mid-morning. Dog, in his enthusiasm, or his efforts to keep busy so he didn't have too much time to think about where he was, had cleared half the slope of brush. There were a lot of green branches stacked six feet high in the bottom of the shaft, along with dry bushes. He thought lighting the pile would make a lot of smoke as well as flames and it would help drive out the last of the snakes from their hiding places. Or suffocate them.

Grant dug six bars out of the glutinous muck that formed the floor near the walls of the tunnel where the gold had spilled out of the old wagons. It was harder work than he'd expected and he threw the bars over near the shallow stream of water formed by the ceiling drips and that which trickled through the tunnel. He would wash off the tarry muck before sending them up in the chain. He unearthed several more powder flasks, fine examples of the old-style embosser's art. He was surprised to hear the gunpowder rattling around inside, apparently still dry, preserved by the spring seals on the pouring spouts. He set the flasks aside: they would restore to original condition with a little work. But all the old guns were rusted and broken, beyond restoration. There were two bent bayonets that he thought he might straighten out for wall decorations, too.

These little diversions held his interest for a time and he had to make himself consciously ignore them so as to concentrate on digging out the gold. They had decided to haul as many bars as they could by noon and then pack up and pull out. It should give them time to clear this devil country by sundown or soon after.

Dog said nothing, but Grant noticed something in the Apache's eyes, a subtle change in his manner, and he knew Dog was mighty appreciative of the thoughtfulness.

It was nearing eleven o'clock when the trouble started.

The first Grant knew about it at the bottom of the shaft was when Sheriff Fergus Perry called down to him and shattered the peaceful little world he and Donna had tried to make here this morning.

'You there, Bronco? We're ready for the next load, so send 'er on up anytime!'

Grant was too stunned to reply right away. What the hell was Perry doing here? 'We'? Who? How many?

Then Perry called again and it all fell into place. 'Feller name of Chick Mundy's with me – you recollect him, don't you?'

Grant did and cursed softly. He should have known Adam Fellows would buy into this, the way he'd set the Denver marshal hassling Perry over the deaths of Barnett and Lewis. No doubt he had a copy of the mesa map, too, and now he'd sent in his hardcases under Chick Mundy to grab the gold.

'Just a reminder, Grant,' Mundy called suddenly. 'I have the Injun and the gal – so start sendin' up that gold.'

Grant drew down a deep breath. 'I've got another lot ready but before I hook it on let me make sure Donna and Dog are OK.'

'Hey, Grant! *We* make the deals!'

Grant waited him out, ignoring the shouted curses, and finally he heard Donna's voice, a little thin and shaky.

'Bronco, they jumped us while we were hauling on the rope. We're all right, though Dog has a sore head. They...'

'*Now* send up that goddamn gold!' Chick sounded angry and Grant hooked on the cradle made out of the bosun's chair.

'Haul away.'

'I want to see your sixgun, belt and the Greener comin' up, too, Grant!'

He knew he had no choice, tied his weapons on to the rope and the whole kit-and-caboodle began to rise in swift, jerky movements.

It seemed a long time before the empty bosun's chair came back down with a couple of gunnysacks attached.

'Tie the sacks to the rope, separate to the chair,' ordered Chick. 'Fill 'em with bars. I want all that gold up here quick as I can.'

'OK, shouldn't take long.'

'The hell does that mean?'

'There aren't many more to come, what else?'

A brief silence and then Chick's voice, sounding real nasty. 'Don't try to pull that on me, you son of a bitch! Mr Fellows *knows* how many bars there are. You'd be a fool to try and hold out. He found out all the details of them wagons, man!'

Grant tried to sound worried. 'I'll have to dig some, then ... only a few just lying around.'

'You find 'em all! Or you'll be seein' that Apache a lot sooner than you think! But you'll only get to see the gal a little at a time – you savvy, Grant?'

Grant figured he had pushed him as far as he dared, loaded a couple of bars into each sack and two on to the chair. He jerked the line twice and watched the load begin to rise. But the lift had hardly begun when there was sudden shouting above, the rattle of gunfire, and a flailing, screaming body plummeted down the shaft, cannoning off the walls several times before smashing into the muddy bottom, crumpling into a shapeless heap.

It had happened so swiftly and un-expectedly that most of the people up top were caught flat-footed.

Blackie, Monaghan and Mailer were

hauling on the ropes when Mailer began complaining that the goddamn Indian ought to be doing some of the donkey work. His companions agreed as they looked at Dog standing near Chick, watched closely by Mexican Jack who had his hands resting on his twin gunbutts. The girl, standing to one side, looked at Dog apprehensively, then Chick grabbed the Indian's arm and shoved him roughly towards the working group.

'Lend a hand,' he growled indifferently.

Dog went easily with the push, dodged around the group straining at the ropes and rammed a shoulder into the startled 'breed. Mexican Jack stumbled into the shaft and screamed all the way down.

The others froze at the unexpectedness of the sudden violence and by that time Dog had grabbed Mailer, yanked him in front of his body and wrenched the man's gun from its holster. He rammed the muzzle against Mailer's spine and fired, holding the slumped body as he triggered again and

Blackie sat down with a grunt, clutching at a bleeding side. The rope hissed and smoked as it whipped back through the pulleys. Donna was unable to move, but then Chick snatched at her as Dog shoved Mailer into Monaghan, spoiling the big man's aim.

Holding the struggling girl with one arm, Chick threw the other out straight and his Colt's muzzle was only a foot from Dog's chest as he dropped hammer. The Apache tried to throw himself aside but twisted violently in mid-air and crumpled on the very edge of the shaft, arms dangling limply. Donna screamed and Chick shook her roughly and turned a snarling face towards Fergus Perry who had come panting in from outside where he had been tending the horses. He skidded to a halt, face pale as he looked at Mailer and Dog and Blackie, now wadding a kerchief over the bullet graze in his side.

'Judas priest! I never counted on no killin'!'

Chick curled a lip, twisted his hand in the back of Donna's hair and made her kneel on the very edge of the shaft. 'Grant!' he bawled.

'What's going on up there?'

'Your Injun made a fool play, Grant!'

'He all right?'

'Dunno – check him out for yourself.'

Donna screamed in horror as Chick stooped quickly, grabbed Dog's moccasined feet and tipped him over the edge of the shaft. Perry groaned and Chick shook the sobbing girl.

'You tell Grant to be sensible or I'll drop you down next, piece by piece!'

Grant watched in horror as the falling body plunged towards him down the shaft. It struck the slackened ropes and they bowed, formed a large loop which briefly hung up the Apache, and the body actually slid down a way with the rope caught around it, slowing the fall a great deal. Then Dog tumbled free again and Grant suddenly ran to the high pile of brush and dragged it hurriedly out into the shaft proper. It teetered and his back creaked but he got it into position and flung himself aside as the Indian crashed into it.

The pile shuddered and branches snapped and cracked and were crushed by the slamming force. But the green brush was springy and absorbed much of the shock before Dog's limp body slid off, almost on top of Grant. He grabbed Dog's arm and dragged him into the mouth of the work tunnel. Panting, he examined the chest wound, grimaced when he saw the scarlet blood frothing around the powder-burned hole and wadded his neckerchief over it as Donna called down the shaft, pleading with him to do what Chick wanted.

'You're dead, Chick! Just as soon's I can get my hands on you!' Grant's rage subsided suddenly as, surprisingly, he detected a faint heartbeat in Dog's chest. Ignoring Chick's shouting from above he examined the Indian quickly. He had a busted arm and maybe one collarbone. Certainly some ribs were gone and the left leg had an awkward bend to it below the knee. But Dog hadn't cannoned off the rocky walls like Mexican Jack whose head had been smashed in even before he reached the bottom. Grant was now wearing the 'breed's twin gun rig but he wasn't sure just what good it was going to do him. He was still crouching over Dog when Chick shouted once again.

'Hey, Grant! Nothin's changed. I've got the gal, you've got what I want!' Donna suddenly screamed. 'I've got my knife under her left ear. If I don't see that load of gold hooked back on the rope in ten seconds, it's gonna come a'flutterin' down to you! Oh, and send up Jack's guns! Thought I'd forgotten 'em, eh?'

'I ain't poking around in that pile of bloody meat for no guns! Judas, I've just been throwing up everything I've ate over the last week!'

Chick's harsh laughter drifted down the shaft. 'All right, we'll get back to the guns.

Just send up the gold. *Now!*"

Grant hooked the gold on the rope that had come away when the load had plunged back down just before Mexican Jack hit. It began to rise jerkily, more slowly than before. He was turning back towards Dog when he heard the rope thrum tautly, more shouting, and he snapped his head up, a hand dropping instinctively to a gun butt. Then his heart slammed up into his throat.

His name echoed down the shaft as Donna screamed it wildly. Startled yells mingled with the sound as he saw she was sliding down the rope, hand over hand, one leg entwined so as to control her rapid descent, even while Chick's men were still trying to haul up. She was gaining, but if she slowed down much she would lose ground and be pulled back towards the surface.

The savagely angry Chick leaned over the edge and triggered two wild shots. They sprayed gravel down the shaft and Grant, aiming carefully so as not to hit the girl, fired back. Chick's head disappeared swiftly as lead chewed the edge.

'Haul up faster! *Faster*, goddamnit!'

Then the girl either slipped or released her grip and suddenly she was falling again, screaming briefly as she snatched at the taut rope. She cried out in pain as her arm was almost torn out of its socket when she managed to find purchase. Her grip slackened and she started to slide down as the rope still rose, Chick cursing the men pulling it up.

'Let go, Donna!' Grant yelled. 'Drop on to the brush-pile! Let *go!*'

She was still about twenty feet high when she found enough courage to release her hold. She plummeted silently through space and moments later crashed into the teetering pile of brush. Grant heard the breath battered from her jerking body as she hit hard, then spilled off sideways, limbs flailing. He caught her awkwardly and ran with her back into the tunnel as Chick began shooting wildly down into the shaft.

He stretched her out alongside Dog and

she moaned, already starting to come out of her daze. She put a hand to the back of her neck and rubbed, then froze when she saw Dog – just as he moaned and rolled his head on to one side, facing her.

'He's still alive!'

'Just barely,' Grant said, and explained the man's injuries quickly.

The girl examined the wound and her teeth tugged at her bottom lip as she looked up at Grant, shaking her head slowly. Then she started to tremble and suddenly hugged herself as if she were cold, only just now realizing what she had done. Her eyes were wide as she looked into Grant's hard-planed face.

'Chick kept saying that as long as he had me, he could force you to do whatever he wanted.' She looked around her, seeing the tunnel and shaft and charred wagon wreckage for the first time. She shivered some more. 'I saw the rope, realized I was still wearing my gloves and ... and next thing I knew I was sliding down.' Her breath seemed to catch in her throat now and she briefly covered her face with her hands showing red and blistered through the tears in the leather gloves. Her voice became a hoarse whisper. 'My God, Bronco, what've I done? Now we're *both* trapped down here!'

They both jumped as Dog suddenly spoke in a rasping whisper. 'No. Bats leave. Must be way out. Follow ... air...'

Grant pressed the cloth firmly over the wound. 'Take it easy, Dog. If there's a way out, I'll find it, and get you to a sawbones.'

Dog's head rolled from side to side and he moaned involuntarily. 'Too late Bronco.' His good hand groped for Grant's, held it weakly. 'You ... best friend. The Soulcatcher bring you to ... my spirit world. We make one long hunt. Just you ... me ... always. I go...'

His last breath came out with that word and Donna choked back a sob. Grant lifted the slack hand, squeezed it between both of his and lay it down by Dog's side. His face was grim as his shoulders slumped. Donna watched, waiting for him to say something, but the only voice she heard was Chick's, drifting down the shaft, followed by a strange, *whooshing* sound...

Several blazing pine-cone torches dropped on to the now scattered brushpile. The dry branches caught almost instantly, blazed up, flames licking the greener brush on top. In seconds, the tunnel was filling with choking smoke.

Grant grabbed the girl and sent her staggering further into the darkness of the work tunnel – the unexplored part. Air flowed from back there somewhere but it wasn't a strong enough current to hold back the smoke which now swirled around them both. They tore strips of cloth from the tails of their shirts' soaked them in water and tied them over their noses and mouths. Grant took down two of the burning lanterns and thrust them into the girl's hands, seeing how small the wick flames were. The oil must be mighty low by now, he thought.

'Take these and go carefully,' he told her, his words muffled by the mask. 'I'll catch up.'

'What ... what're you going to do?'

'Bring Dog. I'm not leaving him here. I'll bury him in the sunshine.'

Lamplight reflected from a brief warmth and softness in her eyes and then she took the lanterns and groped her way forward, breathing raggedly as the shadows leapt and clawed at her.

Bent almost double with his burden, Grant followed, stumbling, feeling the heat on his back, eyes streaming and throat and lungs afire with the roiling smoke. The tunnel became lower, narrower, more airless...

Far behind, he could just make out Chick's voice as the man shouted and taunted, then even that was cut off as he rounded a bend and almost fell over the girl as she crouched ahead of him. She turned to look at him over her shoulder and he saw how white her face was as she held up a lantern. Its feeble glow showed the solid rock wall of a dead-end not a yard away...

Up top, Chick Mundy, face tight with barely contained rage, looked over the edge of the shaft, coughing a little in the rising smoke. He swung back to the others, Perry standing well back, eyeing the man warily.

'The fire's burned down to a heap of red-hot embers now. Blackie, you and Monaghan get on down there after 'em. They'll be trapped in the tunnel, maybe even dead from the smoke.'

'And maybe they're not dead,' Monaghan said, but he checked his sixgun just the same.

'Then you fix it!' Chick snapped, glaring as Blackie started to protest about his wound. 'Shut up!' Chick's Colt menaced them both. 'Get that chair up here and Perry and me'll lower you down. *Now!*'

Miserably, Monaghan and Blackie started hauling up the bosun's chair and Perry released a quiet sigh of relief.

For a moment there he'd thought Chick was going to send him down there into the bowels of the earth.

It wasn't a wall of rock after all.

The fading light of the lantern had only given that impression. It was a wall of clay that barred their way, the surface wriggling with cracks like rivers marked on a map. Air blew through some of those cracks but Grant knew there had to be a bigger hole to allow the bats to escape.

He looked up and found it above their heads: a ragged hole about six inches in diameter through solid rock that sucked at the smoke that still filled the tunnel. He knew with sinking belly that they could never hope to widen that hole without the aid of dynamite...

Which left the clay wall. He pushed his face tight up against one of the widest cracks, cursed as dust got in his eye, hurriedly blinked it out and looked again.

'Think there's light beyond there. Wall

looks to be a couple of feet thick. Likely plugged up this tunnel during one of the floods. We've got to dig through it, Donna.'

Above the muddy rags that still covered her lower face he could read the fear in her eyes. Nonetheless she asked practically, 'What with?'

There was nothing ready to hand that would do. He looked at Dog, thinking he might still have his hunting knife on his belt but the sheath was empty. He listened for any signs of pursuit, knowing Chick would send men down after the smoke cleared. It was still difficult to breathe and he noticed how the girl's chest heaved with each intake of air.

Then he remembered the bayonets.

'Wait here,' he said, before he realized how stupid a remark it was. 'Be back in a minute.'

He left her with both sputtering lanterns and groped along the tunnel walls, crouching low, hunting cleaner air untainted by smoke which was clearing slowly as it was sucked up the air vent in the roof at the dead-end.

Pale light showed ahead, outlining the tunnel entrance under the shaft. He saw the glowing pile of embers from the fire and it painted the mouth of the opposite tunnel the colour of blood. Grant had only ventured in there once, going in just a few feet before he saw that it sloped down steeply towards blackness and the sound of running water far below, some dark, deep-flowing underground river.

Then he heard the squeaking of the pulleys as he crouched beside the small pile of powder flasks, the two bayonets resting on top. He rammed the bayonets through his belt and drew one of the Colts as two men dropped down the shaft on the rope. He didn't know the man with the black beard, but he recognized Monaghan. Both men held guns in their hands.

They saw him at the same time and started shooting instantly. Grant returned their fire, ducking as lead ricocheted into the tunnel behind him. The killers ran for the mouth of the other tunnel and he triggered three fast shots. Monaghan stumbled, one arm dangling limply, righted himself and fired with his good hand as he ducked into the darkness of the tunnel mouth. Blackie shot twice and Grant reeled as stone chips tore one side of his face.

They both raked his tunnel mouth as he lay prone. He hitched himself closer to the wall and his hand felt the five copper powder flasks. He was on his knees at once, emptying his gun with one hand, scooping up the flasks with the other. One by one he tossed them into the thick pile of glowing embers, turned and started to run back down his own tunnel.

Lead buzzed around him as he stumbled, caught a glimpse of the remaining gold bars he'd had ready for taking up, and figured this would be the last time anyone would ever see them...

He was halfway back to the bend when the powder flasks blew, fire erupting in the crumbling shaft.

It wasn't the biggest explosion he'd ever heard but the tunnel concentrated the blastwave and he was knocked sprawling, ears ringing. He banged his head, rolled and twisted around in time to see the tunnel mouth collapsing, the roof coming down like a waterfall of rocks – rushing towards him as they filled the space. He pushed to his feet and started to run, doubled-over, dust swirling around, choking, stinging, blinding. Pieces of the roof above him flaked away and he was showered with fist-sized lumps. He staggered, coughing rackingly, cannoned off the wall of the bend and rolled around, falling over Dog's spread legs as he glimpsed the startled girl in the dim light.

Behind him, there was a sudden, deafening silence and he wiped grit out of his eyes, still coughing, but seeing that the cave-in had stopped several feet short of their sanctuary. A single head-sized piece of rock clattered down.

He saw the girl's mouth move but he

couldn't hear her, his ears still ringing wildly from the explosion. He pulled the bayonets out of his belt, handed her one with a shaking hand as he told her what had happened. He couldn't even hear himself speak and when Donna realized he was deafened, she turned to the wall of clay and began digging alongside him.

The clay was rock hard at first, then softened and came away in large clods that they could lever out. There were broken twigs and branches and other wood that had been caught up by the floods but which had now rotted. These made pockets where it was possible to tear out great chunks with their bare hands. They felt more and more fresh air on their faces as sweat soaked their weary bodies and their muscles ached and cracked.

Neither had any idea how long it took for them to break through but, suddenly, a head-sized lump fell *away* from under their stabbing blades and with the flood of warm air came a blinding flash of sunlight.

The girl fell prone, but Grant lay on his back and kicked the edges of the hole, widening it. He pulled Donna alongside him and pointed to the short tunnel they had broken into. It opened on to the mountainside, framing a patch of blue Colorado sky. No doubt it looked like just another cave from out there.

'Go,' he croaked, pushing her towards the opening. 'Go on out and I'll bring Dog.'

Her eyes were dulled with fatigue and strain, but suddenly she smiled and brushed her lips across his muddy cheek as she climbed through and sucked in a deep lungful of clean, fresh air. She began stumbling towards the far end and Grant slid back to where he had left Running Dog propped against the wall.

'Soon have you out of here, old friend,' he murmured, struggling to get a good grip on the Apache. 'Out in sunlight and away from the demons that haunted you...'

He pushed Dog through, followed and lifted him on to his aching shoulders and walked on unsteady legs towards the sunlight where the girl was waiting.

But she wasn't alone when he stepped out on to the mountainside.

Fergus Perry held Donna in front of his big body while Chick Mundy stood to one side, a cocked sixgun covering Grant. He grinned tightly, triumphantly.

'Just stand like that, holdin' the Injun,' he ordered. 'You are *one* tough bastard, Grant, you know that? Yeah, you know, all right. Wonderin' how we got here, huh?'

Grant nodded, trying not to sag under Dog's weight. The girl was held firmly by the big sheriff.

'You son of a bitch. I dunno how you blew that tunnel but the whole damn shaft collapsed into it, fell right away from under our feet. Had to run for our lives. And saw smoke and dust spewin' outa the hillside here. Knew it had to be another way out, so we come and just waited...'

'What's it matter, Chick?' Grant said tiredly. 'We all lost. The gold's buried now, even the stuff we brought up if the shaft collapsed like you said.'

'Oh, it did. But that only blocked the tunnel from that side. You came out *this* side, so now you can go back in there and bring me out the gold!'

'Chick, there's a whole mountain sitting on top of that gold! The tunnel's blocked almost to the end.'

Chick's jaw was hard, knotted as he bit down. 'Grant, I need that gold. Adam Fellows wants it and if I get it for him I'll get Barnett's old job. Sky's the limit after that. So, somehow, you're *gonna dig that gold outa there!*'

Grant saw there was no reasoning with the man: he was obsessed with getting into Fellows' good books. He made his legs buckle a little and then grunted and swayed, quickly lowering Dog to the ground. He was side-on to the wary Chick and, as he straightened, he dived headlong across the slope, palming up one sixgun, shooting while still airborne. But Chick was fast, dodged sideways, gun blazing as he tripped and slid down the slope, Grant's lead kicking stones around him. Grant hit a patch of scree and went sliding downslope towards the floundering Chick, his gun held out ahead of him, working hammer and trigger, Colt bucking and roaring until empty.

Chick's body jerked and rolled, almost sat up, then flopped back, shirt torn and bloody, face a mess of red meat and white bone. Grant staggered up, realized he was holding an empty gun, and spun towards Perry. The sheriff still held the girl tight against him, his gun at her head

'What's the point, Fergus?' Grant panted. 'There's no gold for anyone now. Let her go. You know if you harm her, I'll come after you and I'll kill you...'

Donna was standing on tiptoe, her face very white beneath the coating of drying mud, her gaze holding steadily to Grant, all her confidence in him. Perry's moon face ran with sweat and suddenly he thrust the girl away from him and holstered his gun.

'Ah, the hell with it. I don't even know what I'm doin' here.' He watched the girl run to Grant and the man slip an arm about her waist, holding her tightly against him. 'But what about Adam Fellows? He usually gets what he wants. He might send some hardcases after us.'

'We'll show 'em the mesa. If they want to dig through a whole damn mountain to try for that gold, then they can.'

Perry nodded but looked dubious. He hesitated, then started across the slope, murmuring something about getting the horses. Grant tilted up Donna's face.

'I need to see to Running Dog. There's a high place on the edge of his own country where he always goes through the ritual of greeting The Four Worlds Of The Apache. I'll be gone maybe a week. Will you wait for me at my ranch? Or in town if you prefer – just so long as you wait.'

She smiled through the filth on her lovely face, tightened her arms about him.

'I'll wait, Bronco. I'll wait...'

This Large Print Book for the partially sighted, who cannot read normal print, is published under the auspices of
**THE ULVERSCROFT FOUNDATION**